YF++

"I can't wait for the next installment. Listen up America, if you want to fall in love with a teen series – pick this one."
Once Upon a Romance.net

"Suspenseful, entertaining, and enthusiastically gruesome, Smith's latest will be lapped up by vampire fans."
The Horn Book

"A true page-turner, I can't imagine any fan of gothic suspense/romance not thoroughly enjoying this – and not just young adult readers either." *Dallas Morning News*

"Smith has built on centuries of vampire lore to create a spooky, snarky, supernatural world all her own." *BookPage*

"Fanpires will not be disappointed with the newest addition to the genre." *VOYA*

"Readers should be hooked by this fully formed world, up through the action-packed finale." *Publishers' Weekly*

"At once glamorous and gruesome... Let the fingers fly through this flowing fantasy." *San Antonio Express-News*

"[A] witty, dark love story of death and redemption."
Booklist

Also by Cynthia Leitich Smith

Tantalize:

"Readers will be tantalized by this dark, romantic, and disturbing fantasy of vampires, werewolves, and a strong no-nonsense heroine. Fans of Stephenie Meyer [...] will eat it up." *School Library Journal*

"Cynthia Leitich Smith is the Anne Rice for teen readers."
Bloomsbury Review

"Werecreatures, vampires, unsolved murders, and more are sure to satisfy readers who lust for blood lore and romance and mysteries." *The Goddess of YA Literature blog*

"Smith juices up YA horror with this intoxicating romantic thriller." *The Horn Book*

"Whether it's the whirlwind plot, the unresolved ending, the fabulous Italian food or all that blood, readers will certainly be licking their lips at the end of *Tantalize*, their appetites whetted for Smith's next enticing adventure."
BookPage

"An impeccably paced suspense story, a sexy romance, and a tough and witty heroine."
Bulletin of the Center for Children's Books

Eternal

Cynthia Leitich Smith

**WALKER
BOOKS**

First published in Great Britain 2009 by Walker Books Ltd
87 Vauxhall Walk, London SE11 5HJ

2 4 6 8 10 9 7 5 3 1

Text © 2009 Cynthia Leitich Smith
Cover Photograph (Man) © Shahn Rowe / Getty Images
Cover Photograph (Wing) © Glenn Mitsui / White / Photolibrary Group

The right of Cynthia Leitich Smith to be identified as author of this
work has been asserted by her in accordance with the
Copyright, Designs and Patents Act 1988

This book has been typeset in Palatino.

Printed and bound in Great Britain by Clays Ltd, St Ives plc

British Library Cataloguing in Publication Data:
a catalogue record for this book is
available from the British Library

ISBN 978-1-4063-2500-3

www.walker.co.uk

For Deborah Noyes

It was the season of Light, it was the season of Darkness,

it was the spring of hope, it was the winter of despair,

we had everything before us, we had nothing before us,

we were all going direct to Heaven, we were all going

direct the other way.

—Charles Dickens, *A Tale of Two Cities* (1859)

Zachary

I MAY BE HEAVEN-SENT, but I'm not perfect.

I watch my girl slip the oversize Dallas Cowboys T-shirt over her pink bikini panties and turn in for the night.

That sounds perverted, I know. But I've always watched her dress, undress, shower, and bathe.

Then there was that one blessed weekend last August when the air conditioner broke. She spent a full day in bed buck naked, reading Tolkien under the ceiling fan.

It's not like I *look* look. Not usually.

What's more, it's my job to keep an eye on her 24/7.

1 ⊙〜

I'm Miranda's guardian angel (GA for short). A newbie created after the first atomic blast in 1945.

Miranda is my second assignment and my reason for being. Not that she has clue one. She can't even see me. Nobody can unless I choose to show myself. That's a no-no. We GAs have our limits. Sure, we help out when we can, but not in any way that's clearly detectable . . . or at least traceable (I'm known to push the limits now and then).

Night after night, I watch her sleep. She's restless. Always restless. I'm forever rearranging the sheets so her legs don't get tangled. Otherwise, she'll wake up.

She doesn't get enough rest as it is. She worries about little mistakes. Or what she frets are mistakes. What other people think of her. What will happen next.

All humans do. I wish they could glimpse infinity. It would make glitches like a C in algebra or a nitpicking parent or being ignored by The Guy feel a whole lot less fatal.

I would love to talk to Miranda. To tell her that.

She woke up crying twice last year around the time of her parents' divorce. I don't know what she dreams about. I've heard that older angels can tap into the mind. Sounds tempting, right? But I wouldn't do that. Or at least I can't.

I'm already so here. Miranda deserves her own mental space.

This is her physical space, though. My fave place on terra firma.

Since she's sound asleep, I risk assuming solid form on a denim beanbag chair, taking it in. Four cream-colored walls, two windows, eight-foot ceilings, outdated gold shag. A twin bed, desk set, tall cedar dresser, and hope chest. The blanket her grandma knitted. The stuffed toy penguin from SeaWorld. The poster of the earth that reads: HOME, SWEET HOME.

Here, I can see the little girl she was. The woman she's turning into.

Miranda began wearing bras like the one hanging off the back of her desk chair in fifth grade. She gave up on the third of her fuzzy pink diaries that same year.

One wall is covered by a bookcase. She reads paper-backs mostly. Lots of series titles. One shelf is jammed full of acting and theater books. The library stack on the desk waits to be returned. The college information packet beside it is from the University of North Texas. The cell phone next to her PC hasn't worked since it went through the wash last weekend.

Beside it rest copies of *A Tale of Two Cities* and *Romeo and Juliet*. Dickens is assigned reading, but Shakespeare is Miranda's ticket to her dream. Today's date is circled in red on the Narnia calendar. Spring-play auditions are this afternoon. My girl is so shy. I'm surprised she signed up.

Mr. Nesbit is taking a drink of water from the bottle attached to his cage. He's good company, for a gerbil.

I dissolve again so I don't have to wiggle up from the

beanbag. It's time to check on Miranda. To breathe in her lemongrass body wash. To study her heart-shaped face. It's something I do almost as often as humans blink.

This time is different. Horrific. I recoil, looking for another explanation. But the ladybug nightlight is still on. The nearly full moon hasn't been eclipsed.

A smoky gray film swirls around Miranda. It clings to her. It twists into long-fingered hands, caressing her cheeks, pawing at her slim neck and shoulders. It lengthens into a translucent sheet, covering her body, sliding up over her head.

It's wrong. It has to be. But I've seen it before.

My girl is sleeping in the shadow of Death.

Miranda

EITHER MY HOUSE IS HAUNTED or my beanbag is possessed. Or maybe they're the same thing, haunting and possession. I'll have to ask my best friend, Lucy. She'll know. Whichever it may be, I swear the denim lump changes shape as I sleep. This morning it's definitely mushier in the middle than it was last night.

"Miranda!" Mom calls. "You're going to be late for school."

As if I don't know that. I grab my black mesh backpack and try to sneak through the foyer and living-dining room, past the kitchen, calling, "Bye!" only to be intercepted by Mom in front of the pantry.

She's wrapped in a thick white robe, her dark hair twisted in a knot. By now, she's usually dressed and ready to sell cosmetics. "You're not eating breakfast?"

I can smell the turkey bacon and burnt toast. I remind myself that Mom tries.

"I don't want you stuffing your face with cookies at school," Mom goes on. "You know how chocolate—"

"My skin is fine." Not flawless, but I'm by no means the "before shot" in the acne commercial. I make a show of checking my watch. "I have to pick up Lucy and—"

"This came yesterday." Mom holds up a postcard, cutting me off. "From your father."

I suppress a sigh, unable to resist taking a look. *Greetings from Alaska!* He's on a luxury cruise. It's news to me, but that's no surprise. He quickly became an every-other-holiday dad, not an every-other-holiday-and-every-other-weekend dad. Because of his job. Because he has to travel. Because he's starting over in his new life.

"He didn't write this," I say before realizing I should've kept my mouth shut.

Mom puts her hands on her hips. "It's a woman's handwriting."

She's right. The letters are big and loopy (*Wish you were here*), nothing like Dad's businesslike, slanted scribble. Mom must've stewed over the postcard all night.

They're divorced, my parents. It's been final for a while. He's allowed, I guess, to go out with someone else.

Still, this is new for us. I always assumed Mom would start dating first, that she'd need the attention. Apparently this morning she needs me.

For the first time, I realize we're the same height now, my mother and me. To cheer her up, I share news that I'd intended to keep a secret. "I'm auditioning for the school play today: *Romeo and Juliet*." As her expression predictably transforms from pinched to rapturous, I open the door to the garage. "It's not a big deal."

"That's . . . It's wonderful!" She clasps her hands together. "You see, I knew you didn't need a shrink!"

It takes me a moment to process that. "You were going to send me to a shrink?" Dad mentioned it once during their separation, but more in an in-case-you-need-someone-to-talk-to kind of way. Not like I was some kind of loser/freak.

"It wasn't my idea." Mom reaches to give me one of her stiff half hugs, right arm at a sharp angle, as if she'll break if she pulls me too close. "Your father's an imbecile, but we already knew that. I told him you were just slow to bloom. Any daughter of mine is destined to be a star!"

I pull free and take the step down into the cold, cluttered two-car garage. My Honda is a don't-hate-me-for-leaving gift from Dad.

"After all," Mom calls from the doorway, "I was Little Miss Bay Area."

Starting the car, I silently mouth along with her, "And Miss San Francisco!"

"Anytime you're ready," Ms. Esposito says from the first row, her clipboard poised and her smile encouraging. She's a first-year teacher, beaming with eagerness.

I shift my weight on the stage as thoughts zoom through my head.

The recently redecorated auditorium (it still has that new-car smell) is mostly empty. The first few rows of the theater are occupied by the other people auditioning—the die-hard drama geeks, plus a few out-of-our-league wannabes like me. Then there's Denise Durant and two of her acolytes. They're more reality-TV than Globe-Theatre material, but they love being in the spotlight.

I wish Lucy were here, but acting isn't her thing. Besides, she's serving an hour of detention right now for accidentally handing in a *Ginger Snaps* fan fic instead of her Government report.

I order myself to breathe. As Grandma Peggy says, life's short, and besides, I'm almost positive that no one has ever actually died from humiliation.

"Anytime," Ms. Esposito repeats, prompting giggles from Denise's row.

I'm reading Juliet, act IV, scene III. We were given an option of doing a monologue (having a shot at a major role), which is how it's always worked in past years, or this, reading with another actor (for those of us who suffer from "audition anxiety").

The latter was the suggestion of our school counselor, who's anxiety-phobic—if you use the words "test" and "anxiety" in the same sentence, she'll immediately book you for a shiatsu spa treatment.

"'What! are you busy, ho? need you my help?'"

I do a double take on the "ho" until my brain clicks that Wayne White has given up on my beginning and moved on. Wayne's perched on a stool, his long, bony limbs bent like a hunched scarecrow. He should've whispered my line instead, but he's probably embarrassed at having to read Lady Capulet.

"'No, *madam!*'" I manage. "'We have cull'd such necessaries / as are behoveful for our state to-morrow ...'" The words are coming, but my body is frozen in place. "'So please you, let me now be left alone ...'" What I wouldn't give to be left alone right now. "'And let the nurse this night'"—I sound okay, but I look like an android on *pause*— "'sit up with you." I take a lurching, Frankenstein-like step to the right.

Ms. Esposito looks like she's worried something's medically wrong with me.

"'For, I am sure, you have your hands full all ...'" All ... All *what*?

I glance at Denise, who's biting her lip to keep from

laughing. Lucy says I shouldn't let her get to me, but ever since kindergarten, whenever Denise is around, it's like a clawed hand is squeezing the blood from my heart.

The Thespians catch my eye. They're nodding along, rooting for me. I've always watched them at school, the way they joke around and color their hair and could care less what anyone thinks of them. Part of the reason I wanted to do this was to become one of them. They're the most alive people here.

I try to relax and fall into my character. I need to be Juliet—romantic, tragic, doomed. "'All . . . in—in—in this so sudden business!'" I fight not to cringe.

Denise isn't trying to stop herself now, despite Ms. Esposito's fierce, "*Shh!*" She's cackling, her and her friends, their laughter punctuated by a snort that doubles them over.

"Oh, my God!" one exclaims. "She's horrible!"

"'Good-night,'" Wayne reads in a monotone, his chin on his hand. "'Get thee . . .'"

I don't hear the rest. Geoff Calvo has entered the auditorium. Five feet, eleven inches of soccer studly-ness, thundering down the center aisle, drawing every eye except Ms. Esposito's. I would say it's not his looks that I'm attracted to, except that we've never had a conversation. I always tell myself it's because I haven't come up with that great opening line yet. The one that will make him smile and see me as if for the first time and cue the swelling background music, just like in the movies. That's the fantasy.

The reality: Geoff strolls to Denise and gives her this disgusting, half-lick kiss on the lips. It's stupid, I decide right then, to "like" someone you don't really know.

When did they start going out, anyway?

" 'F-farewell!' " I sputter. " 'God knows when we shall meet again.' "

"Kill me now," I plead that evening, ducking behind the nearest DVD display as a couple of Thespians swing through the shop, returning rentals. "Or better yet, let's go."

"Relax, they're already gone." Lucy slings an arm around my shoulders, leading me away from the CHICK FLICK section of the brightly lit store. "Besides, they don't like Denise's clique any more than we do."

This afternoon, when Lucy found me crying in the girls' bathroom at school, she was all big hugs and "Who needs 'em?" and "Everything will be all right."

Lucy's never been one for wallowing, though. She's ready to move on. "Now, now, weary traveler," she says. "There is no shame in this journey. Among the dateless, movie night is a time-honored tradition."

"On Valentine's Day?" I ask, as if that hasn't been our plan the past few years running.

We're at Movie Magic the night before V-Day, while there's still some selection. Or at least that's Lucy's theory.

I also suspect my favorite Scream Queen is here hoping to, well, check out the checkout guy. For the last few months, he's been her third favorite topic after Neil Gaiman and whatever she's up- or downloaded most recently on the Internet.

"Oh, woe is Miranda!" she exclaims, forcibly upbeat.

When I don't banter back, she tilts her head, and her expression grows more serious. "You seem . . . Is anything else wrong? Anything really fatal?"

I debate telling Lucy that my dad is in Alaska (or at least floating on a boat around it) with some mysterious woman who's forging his postcards, that my mom is in the midst of one of her trademark needy phases because of it, and that she may sign off on sending me to a shrink after I tell her about today's audition.

"My beanbag is possessed," I reply instead.

"Interesting." At HORROR, Lucy holds up *The Grudge.* "What do you think?"

We've seen it before. That said, I love movies. Lucy and I have been watching films and munching popcorn— with real butter—on her L-shaped sectional almost every weekend for as long as I can remember, and last summer, my job was working concession at the mall multiplex. "I think—"

"Can I help you ladies find something spooky?" It's Lucy's crush, "Kurt," a fact we deduced early on due to the helpful plastic name tag on his red polo-style shirt.

He's tall, taller than Lucy—which, for her, is key—a sandy blond, and looks a couple of years older than us. Despite the safety pin stuck through his right nostril, he's remarkably cute for a DVD rental guy.

Lucy decides to take their flirtation to the next level. "I'm Lucy," she says, extending a hand, "and this is Miranda. I don't think we've officially met."

He smiles with perfect teeth, shakes her hand and mine. "I know. Your names and addresses are in the computer."

I blink at that, but Lucy is unfazed. "What we're looking for tonight," she says, "is more of a real-life adventure. When do you get off?"

He laughs, my jaw drops, and even the overhead fluorescents seem to dim.

"I get off . . ." He pauses long enough to make the bad joke, but not so long that it's crude. Almost. "At eleven. But it's a school night, right?"

"No classes tomorrow," Lucy explains. "District conferences."

Kurt frowns briefly at that like he's never heard of such a thing. "Well then, if y'all are up for it, I have a scary idea."

Whoa. How did I get dragged into this? "Me?" I say. "I, um, I have curfew at —"

"You're spending the night," Lucy cuts in. She tells Kurt, "My parents trust me, and they're sound sleepers."

"Bitchin'," he replies, taking the movie from her and setting it back on the shelf. "Me and this friend of mine, sometimes we kick back a few brews at that old cemetery by the high school. You know the one I mean?"

We do. Lucy has this freakish fascination with graves. She'll walk around cemeteries with paper and colored pencils and make impressions of the border designs engraved in the tombstones. She'll read the names and dates and try to guess how people died.

"I love the place," she admits. "They say the dead walk there at midnight."

I don't know who "they" are, but that isn't information I appreciate.

Kurt laughs again. "We'll meet you and the dead after work."

Zachary

"KILL ME NOW," Miranda says at the video store.

If an invisible angel could cringe, I would. She's upset about her parents and the audition, I get that. Normally I'd be all over trying to find a way to make her feel better.

I love Miranda. I do. But this evening, my girl's adolescent crisis of the week means exactly jack. The last thing we need right now is to tempt Fate.

The shadow still covers her face like a veil, her hands like gloves, and trails after her like a bridal train.

Sure, I know the score. There comes a day when every GA has to let go. I understand that when the time comes, she'll be joyfully welcomed upstairs by Grandpa Shen and everyone she knows who gets there first. But life is such a gift. Such a blessing. At only seventeen, she's barely had a chance to breathe it in. To make whatever difference she can in this world. Her dream of becoming an actress. Growing into a woman who can command center stage. She deserves her moment in the spotlight. She deserves that and more.

Nothing is destined. Miranda's free will can alter her future. Circumstances can change. She doesn't have to die. Shadow or no shadow, I'm not about to give up on her.

"Can I help you ladies find something spooky?" Kurt asks.

What's Lucy saying? What is she thinking? She's an ongoing challenge, the X factor in Miranda's life. I'm the one who has to field damage control.

It was Lucy who led her last summer in sneaking into an apartment complex so they could soak in the Jacuzzi. It was me who kept the residents of the three units over-looking the pool busy with overflowing bathtubs and ant infestations and toddler reading time so they didn't hap-pen to glance out their windows.

It was Lucy who sent a JPEG of Miranda's sophomore-year photo to an Internet predator in Fort Worth, think-ing he was a high-school varsity wrestler from Houston. It was me who infected his system with a virus and made their ISPs incompatible.

Now here's Kurt. And what about him? He's been a

bit player in their lives for months. I've never paid much attention to him. Mistake?

I materialize low behind the counter, staying out of sight, and search through the stack of Movie Magic paperwork for clues. I'm quick to find the employee directory under a wadded-up McDonald's bag and skim the short list until I see the name.

Kurt Brodecker. He lives in the West End.

"If y'all are up for it," Kurt says. "I have a scary idea."

Oh, I'm hating the sound of that. I look for a display to tip. A fire alarm to pull.

"Me?" Miranda chimes in. "I, um, I have curfew at—"

"You're spending the night," Lucy interrupts. "My parents trust me, and they're sound sleepers."

The cemetery? Dark. Secluded. Sprawling. Yikes.

"They say the dead walk there at midnight," Lucy claims.

In the bright fluorescent light, the shadow shudders and darkens around my girl.

Miranda

LUCY AND I DON'T SAY ANOTHER WORD until we leave the store, get in my car, and crank the heater.

"Cemetery?" I exclaim. "I don't do cemeteries. Not at night. Not with strange boys. Not with brews."

Brews. Bitchin'. Who talks like that?

Now that I think about it, what do we really know about Kurt? "What if he's an axe-murdering film geek?" I add. "Didn't you *watch* any of those movies you made us rent?"

Lucy puts on her seat belt like it's nothing. "You liked *Van Helsing*."

"I liked Hugh Jackman in that black hat and long coat." I lower the volume on the Christian rock station. "I know you're all about the creepy fantastic, but it's not like there aren't real-world monsters. Shifters—"

"Werepeople," she says. "God, Miranda, don't be such a bigot."

I let the "bigot" thing slide. Every news story I've ever seen about a werewolf or Bear or Cat or whatever has involved a body count. But Lucy can get loud and political, and I'm not up for it tonight.

I don't tell her what's really bugging me. That my day has been lousy and that she promised a comforting movie night and now she's dragging me along so she can hook up with some guy. I'm disappointed in myself and the world and her, too. "What about vampires?" I ask, pulling out of the strip-mall parking lot. "This is Dallas after all."

"That was a hundred years ago," Lucy says.

It was more like 1963, the last known public sighting of a vampire in Texas, and on the grassy knoll, no less. "But vampires can live forever, right? He, I mean, it—"

"Vampires don't *live* at all," she points out, "and neither do we."

She has me there. "Fine, I'll go. But when Kurt leads his minions in a march around the cemetery with our heads on sticks, don't say I didn't warn you."

Miranda

"MAYBE SOMETHING CAME UP," I say, fiddling with my cardigan. It's cold enough in mid-February that there are patches of ice on the ground, and we've been parked outside Chrysanthemum Hills Cemetery for over forty-five minutes.

"Maybe they're waiting inside," Lucy counters. "It's not like we discussed exactly where to meet. We should just head on in."

"Wait!" I say, but she's already getting out of the car.

The cemetery was here before the high school and the subdivisions surrounding it. A few years back, after some highly publicized incidents of "trespassing and desecration" (kind of an overstatement for empty beer bottles and cigarette butts), the rock wall surrounding the property was doubled in height and barbed wire was strung along the top.

I have no idea how Kurt or Lucy think we're getting past the locked gate.

I grab my purse, even though she left hers under the front passenger seat. I don't have my cell with me because last week it died a watery death, but Lucy's is in her trench-coat pocket.

Why did I ever let her talk me into watching all those zombie movies? I can't help thinking of the rotting bodies beneath the earth beyond the wall—their decomposing hands breaking through their caskets, clawing through the dirt, their decomposing heads rising through the soil, their gaping mouths eager to gobble our brains.

"There's a note." Lucy unties a thin black ribbon securing a rolled piece of paper to the wrought-iron gate.

The security chains have been unwrapped and tossed to the ground.

I shiver. "What happened to the padlock?"

Lucy is too busy to care. With one hand, she holds the note to the moonlight. "We're supposed to meet them at the mausoleum across from the tallest angel. Romantic, don't you think?"

I don't. I don't think that spooky is sexy.

"The tallest angel," she muses. "That's the one at the Carton family plot. It's clear on the other side of the grounds." The rusty gate swings open. Jogging, she calls, "Come on, we should hurry."

I have no choice but to follow. "Lucy!"

"What?" she yells, and her voice sounds loud in the dead place.

It startles me into stopping, and I realize I almost stepped on a large bat. It's flopping on the wet ground. I'm not sure if it's sick or if one of its wings is broken. I know better than to touch it, rabies and all.

"What's wrong?" She jogs back to fetch me. "Oh."

"I think it's hurt."

"Just leave it. You don't want to get bitten, do you?"

I don't. "Maybe we should call somebody, like animal control."

"You call animal control. I'm going on my date." Lucy walks off again.

Underneath that attitude, I tell myself, she isn't trying to be impossible. She's just nervous about hanging out with older guys, especially Kurt.

I hesitate, unable to stop staring at the distressed animal on the brown grass. When I look up, Lucy is lost among the bare trees and gray tombstones.

My fear edges up a notch. I abandon the bat.

The other side of the cemetery, she said. I can find that.

It's like the statues are watching, larger than life,

frozen in time, angels mostly. Crosses rise across the landscape. Some freestanding, others etched in stone.

Tuesday night's ice storm savaged the trees, breaking limbs, splitting the trunk of a century-old oak.

The paved entry splits into three gravel roads, and I choose the one in the middle, unwilling to step on a grave until I have to. What kind of freaks meet girls in cemeteries?

"Lucy!" I search for the angel statue she mentioned.

As I stray from the path, the historic cemetery is eerie in its silence. A cloud shrouds the moon. I keep going, reminding myself of how Lucy stuck up for me in the middle school girls' locker room when Denise mocked my double-A bra, how Lucy was beyond supportive when Mom and Dad imploded, and how she sat through two seasons of varsity soccer so I could drool over Geoff. What a waste of time he was.

I walk on, despite the deepening darkness, determined to find my friend.

Zachary

WHERE DID LUCY TAKE OFF TO? I could rise again, but the bat was a close call. I briefly took flight for an overhead view, and Miranda was almost bitten.

Now I know better than to let her out of my sight—period. The whole universe is in play. I have to guard Miranda tonight like never before. I have to protect her.

As we make our way, I slow my long stride to match hers.

When she leaves the gravel path, I relocate to the stone platform of a life-size angel statue. It's a good likeness of Raphael, though the nose is chipped, and the real Raphie is four inches taller. The monument is substantial, though.

There's room enough for me to stand comfortably on the base. I'm some distance away but directly in Miranda's path. From here, I can see her as well as more of the surrounding landscape.

From this angle, I spot the gaping hole. A newly dug grave. The cemetery has been closed since the storm. The usual precautions haven't been taken. Lucy is nowhere in sight. Neither is Kurt. Miranda is too busy looking for them to glance down.

She's going to fall! This is it. I just know it. I clench my fists, desperate to help. What's a voice in the darkness? A light in the distance? What could it hurt?

"Stay back!" I call out, taking solid form. "Miranda!" Stretching my wings, I illuminate the scene.

My girl stumbles. But at the last moment, she throws her hands out. She's safe! Safe. I've saved her.

Miranda

"STAY BACK!" someone warns. It's a man's voice, not a boy's. "Miranda!"

Then a burst of light blinds me. I squint, raising my hand to shield my eyes. It's too big, too bright. My first thought makes no sense—a bird? No, it's the figure of a guy in the light, of the light. Stupid me, it's a guy *with* a light, standing in front of the tallest angel statue. He isn't Kurt. Who is he? How does he know my name?

I take a tentative step forward and stumble, barely catching myself from plunging into an open grave. If I'd fallen in, I could've broken my neck.

As I push up from the ground, someone screams in the distance. Lucy? Lucy!

I dart behind the nearest crypt, seeking refuge in its deep, thick shadow.

What direction did the scream come from?

I take a step back, another, only to collide with a second man. I yelp, and my first fleeting thought is that an awful lot of people are hanging out at the cemetery tonight.

With relief, I realize it's probably Kurt—it must be, and the guy with the light is his friend. They're playing a stupid joke, trying to scare me and Lucy.

Cool, dry hands clamp my forearms, and the man turns me so we can peer at each other in the darkness. He's towering, debonair. His fair, sharp features look as if they were etched in chalk. He's not Kurt, not anyone Kurt would hang out with, and too finely dressed to be a groundskeeper or security guard.

The stranger's eyes glint red, a trick of the moonlight, and when I open my mouth, nothing comes out. I try to free myself, but it's no use. My body won't cooperate. I don't know why. I don't know what's wrong with me.

Then the stranger's eyes glint red again, and I forget myself. I forget Lucy. I forget angels. The light is gone. The shadow has seized me.

My veins contract at the formal, slightly southern voice.

"Good evening," he says.

Zachary

WHERE DID SHE GO?

Without bothering to make myself ethereal again, I take two steps in the direction of where I last saw Miranda. Then a blow to the back of my head knocks me to the ground. Pain shoots through the base of my skull.

"What have you done?" a resounding voice demands.

Holy crap! It's Michael. The archangel. The Sword of Heaven. The Bringer of Souls. He must've just used the hilt of his sword to strike me down.

"You know better than to reveal yourself!" he thunders. "And in full glory! You changed the natural order. You bid the fiend in."

"Fiend?" I shift, confused, off-balance. From the other side of the stone wall, I hear a car door shut. Another. "I—"

"Miranda Shen McAllister should be in my charge now," Michael declares as an engine starts, "my care, and now her very soul is forfeit."

I hear wheels turning on wet pavement. "I—"

"You have interfered in a way you should not have," Michael scolds, "and you will *both* pay the penalty." With that, he vanishes as if he's wasted enough time with me.

I can't hear the car, not anymore.

Have I fallen? I must have fallen. Fallen in love. Fallen from grace.

The archangel, my wings, and my girl are gone.

Zachary

A CRY FOR HELP rips into the night. It's Lucy, Miranda's best friend in the world. I ignore the throbbing of my skull. I run.

I'm clumsy in my solid, wingless form. I trip in my sandals over a fallen branch. Skid against the hard dirt, tearing off skin on my palms and knees and chin. My white robes are wet and dirty.

Tonight is my first experience with physical pain. With cold. They pale against the heartache. I pray that when the monster took Miranda, it didn't hurt her too much.

I stand and listen. After a moment, I hear a male voice. It's soft. It's convincing. It's coming from off to the west. I pick my steps more carefully. Seconds later, I vault over a low arched tombstone and into a clearing.

Kurt bares his fangs, releases Lucy's throat, and bolts into the darkness.

I swallow hard, having seen for myself what he is.

Knowing what that means for my girl.

Lucy coughs. "Miranda," she chokes out. "You have to find Miranda."

It takes a moment to register that it's me Lucy is talking to. I'm used to seeing her. But I'm not used to her seeing me.

I'm not sure why, in the midst of all this, she trusts me to be on her side. Maybe it's because I appear to have frightened away her attacker. Maybe it's intuitive or helped by a nudge from Lucy's guardian angel, whoever that is.

In any case, she's right. Despite what's just happened, I still need to track down Miranda.

I'm no expert. Only the Big Boss is all-knowing, and GAs don't usually deal with evil this close to the source. But I do know that the transformation from human to the living dead takes about a month unless the subject dies first, which triggers an immediate change. The clock starts ticking once unholy blood is digested (transfusions work, too). However tainted, Miranda may still be human. She may be suffering.

"Can you walk?" I ask.

Lucy plants her boots and then sways. "I'm all right. I'm all right."

She's shaking. We're both sweating. The chill is brutal.

"You're the hero," she whispers. "If there are monsters, there must be heroes. You're the hero, right? You're magical, right? You frightened away the vampire."

Vampire. It's wretched to hear that word out loud.

"No normal person would be dressed like that," Lucy insists.

I realize then how strange I must look to her in the standard uniform—the long white sleeveless robe and sandals, especially since the temperature is in the mid-40s.

"You'll help me save Miranda, won't you?"

"She's not here," I say, supporting Lucy's forearm. "They took her."

On the way out, I snag Miranda's purse from a flat tombstone.

Back at the Honda, I fish out the car keys, cash card, and phone card. Lucy uses her cell phone to call 911. By the time she signs off, the car heater is blasting.

"I have to go," I say. I hate to, but the authorities will arrive any minute. I can only imagine what they'd make of me. "Don't worry. I'll keep watch until help comes."

"No! We have to go *now*. Miranda needs us."

Lucy's face is splotchy. By morning, her throat will be bruised from Kurt's grip, but the skin is mercifully unbroken. He must've just caught her when I found them.

"The cops can't h⸱⸱   ⸱cy wipes away a
tear. "Not reall⸱   ⸱er, though. Kurt
drives ⸱   ⸱ck. Tell them
⸱⸱   and . . ."

⸱ since they
⸱ach other
⸱ring in
⸱ues."
⸱ out

o⸱

ute.   ⸱ape
it as b⸱

"Be   ⸱e the stone wall. If
you're no⸱   ⸱ m coming after you."

There's   ⸱⸱randa admired so much. While
Lucy's distra⸱   ⸱y the 911 operator, I put some distance
between myself and the Honda. A couple of moments
later, I duck behind a shrub as an ambulance and two
squad cars zoom by.

Michael was right to yank my wings. To toss me out of
the fold.

Last night I shouldn't have shown myself to Miranda.
Not in full glory. Not at all. If I hadn't, she would've
died in that grave. My girl's soul would've been carried

upstairs by the archangel himself. Her arrival would've been celebrated.

I didn't know what would happen. I thought losing her then, so young and soon, was total BS. Didn't I? Did I stop to think at all?

So I bent one rule. It was my instinct, my duty, to protect her. Besides, didn't she deserve a little happiness here on terra firma?

After all those years of watching her, watching over her, it never crossed my mind that she'd be afraid of me. I always assumed that knowing for sure about angels, knowing she had one of her own, would make her feel better.

In the end, the loss was worse than I ever imagined.

After leaving Lucy in the hands of the rescue pros, I hiked a couple of miles to a twenty-four-hour gas station. I used Miranda's cash card at the ATM, emptying the $532 account, and her phone card to call a cab. I kept the coat lapels pulled high and stood at an angle to avoid any cameras.

Then I spent the night at a mission shelter, where I picked up a change of clothes, and took a bus here this morning.

I'd wanted to come right away. But I had a delayed physiological reaction to my powers being revoked. It first hit when I was waiting for the taxi. I could barely stand, and I was achy, feverish, and dizzy most of the night. By dawn, though, I began to feel better—physically at least.

Right now, I'm in an alley, casing the four-story red brick building at Kurt's address. Supposedly, vamps are weaker in the daylight, not that it'll matter much if they're indoors.

I guess the West End makes sense for them, location-wise. It's probably a good hunting ground. Miranda and Lucy were here last summer for the Taste of Dallas food festival.

I don't know what I'll do if I find Miranda. I don't think there's a cure. But I can try. Maybe something like an exorcism would work.

My stomach clenches at the smell of smoking meat from a nearby barbecue restaurant. For the first time, I'm weak from hunger. But I won't back down. This building is the only lead I've got. Should I wait? See if she comes out? Should I—

An explosion rocks the ground beneath me.

I dive for cover behind an open Dumpster. I rip open the scab on my chin and slam my shoulder into a sharp metal corner, tearing Lucy's coat. At least I'm shielded from the heat, the falling brick and raining glass.

Once the wreckage stills, I don't wait for the smoke to clear. I stumble—right arm bent over my head, left sleeve in front of my nose and mouth—into the street. I crunch debris beneath the soles of my sandals.

The fourth floor, Kurt's floor, is on fire. Is he up there? Is Miranda?

A second explosion knocks me back down. Car alarms wail. I hear a siren. Smoke billows—dense, blinding. Nothing could've survived that blast.

Someone beat me here. Vampire hunters or shifters or who knows what.

My money is on a shifter group. Werewolves, werehogs, take your pick. The Big Boss loves variety. Elk have been more proactive lately.

There's no way to know for sure.

I swallow the thin hope I had of minimizing the damage I've done, the destruction of my Miranda. If she was up there, I try to tell myself, maybe this is mercy. She was a sweet, loving girl. She wouldn't have wanted to go on like that.

Staggering from the scene, I remember that it's Valentine's Day.

Missing Miranda

CANDLELIGHT VIGIL TONIGHT

The purpose of this blog is to let people know that they should be looking for my best friend, Miranda Shen McAllister. She has been missing since February 13.

She was last seen that night at Chrysanthemum Hills Cemetery, which is near Midland Heights High School in Dallas.

Miranda may be with a tall blond guy in his late teens/ early twenties. He may have a safety pin stuck through his nose. He may be driving a maroon Lexus, and he may go by the name Kurt. He used to work at Movie Magic in the Midland Heights neighborhood, but he hasn't shown up there since February 13.

You may have heard a rumor that Miranda ran away from home. That's not true. She was having a bad day, but I was with her that night. She didn't want to go out at all. I'm positive that she's been kidnapped.

Besides, even if Miranda did run away, she could still be in real danger.

There's going to be a candlelight vigil at seven tonight at the MHHS football field. If you're in the area, please come. If not, again, please keep your eyes open for Miranda. She could be anywhere by now.

Click here for a slideshow of photos of Miranda. Click here for a banner you can put on your site. Click here for a PDF of a "Missing Teen" flyer with Miranda's picture on it.

Posted by savemiranda at 7:43 AM   Post 1 of 1

Comments   Link

Miranda

I DREAM OF BLACK-AND-BLUE BUTTERFLIES, slicing pain, pleasure pounding.

I dream of star flying and soft leather, of drowning, my gums heavy, muscles numb, and throat raw. I'm lost among the tombstones, swallowed by the moon.

"Can't breathe, can't breathe," I whisper, shifting bare-skinned on slippery silk. The room smells of lavender and talcum powder, roses and cigars. A Johnny Cash song plays at low volume. "Can't . . ."

"You don't have to, sugar," answers an unfamiliar masculine voice. "It's time to open your eyes. We're all so tickled to meet you."

I try, I do. It's hard to form words. It hurts. "Can't . . ."

"Easy there, drink this," he says.

I take the straw at my lips. I sink into the salty black-berry warmth, the not-caring place. I don't know who he is. A doctor, I'd say, but do doctors call you "sugar"? I don't think so. I'm not anyone's sugar, anyone's girl. I hardly have any friends except—

"Lucy!" My eyes open, and I struggle to sit. "Where's Lucy?"

The cool hand on mine is reassuring. The other has taken my cup away. The formally dressed man attached to both is movie-star striking, the hollows of his cheeks accented by flickering candlelight from the candelabra in the far corners of the room. His Asian-style chair is pulled to the edge of my iron-framed canopy bed. "Not to fret, your friend is safe. You have my word."

The room is bigger than Lucy's entire condo. Heavy pink-and-black-checked drapes cover the arched windows. They match the bedding.

Pink and white roses, lilies, and orchids in crystal vases crowd every antique surface. More cascade to the hardwood floor.

My wrists are bruised as if I've given blood or had a transfusion or been restrained. Or all three.

I've gone crazy. It's the only explanation. This is no average storefront shrink. My parents have sent me to the Club Med of insane asylums. "I'm . . . Who are you?"

"My name is Archibald Mosby Radford, originally of the Virginia Radfords by way of eastern Mississippi, western Oklahoma, and Toronto. According to custom, you're welcome to call me 'Master' or 'Majesty' or 'Father.' I'd prefer 'Daddy,' to tell the truth, but I'm sad to say it's falling out of favor. There's no need to fuss. You remember me, sugar. I'm the one who saved you that night in the cemetery."

I remember the cemetery. I remember the light.

"You've got what folks these days are calling 'post-traumatic stress,'" he adds. "It's like a hangover from what you were before."

Before I can process that, a matronly woman in an apron appears outside the open doorway. "Pardon me, sir."

"Quickly, Nora," the man spits out. "The medicine is wearing off. What's the trouble?"

"The aristocracy has gathered outside in the snow beneath the windows," she replies. "They're waiting to see her. Harrison is handing out blood by the bucket."

I'm standing. I don't know how it happened. I don't care. I like the feel of the bare wood on my bare feet. I'm naked. I don't care about that either. I hear the blood slipping through the woman's body, feeding her heart. It's quicker now, the heartbeat.

I'm moving fast. I'm not used to this speed. I slide on a round wool rug and miss my target. The woman. Nora. My palms hit the stone wall, my clawlike fingernails break. My head falls forward, and the impact feels like it cracked my skull.

Liquid snakes through my hair and runs down my cheeks. My tongue darts to taste. It's my blood I'm drinking.

The woman, Nora, she's filled with more. Only hers is warm.

Why doesn't she run? Why do I want her to?

I know the answer, and it stops me in place. On some level, I've known since I woke up. All those monster movies Lucy made me sit through. My broken nails. The right pinkie nail is curved and an inch long. I feel my fangs with my fingers and puncture the tip of my tongue on each. Blood rises, salty and seductive.

I recall the radiant man . . . last night . . . was it last night? . . . in the cemetery. Why didn't the butterflies save me?

No, he saved me. The other one. The doctor? The one with me now. That's what he said.

A delusion—it's the most reasonable explanation. I'm sick. That's why I've been checked into this mental hospital.

Suddenly, I'm caught, tangled and restrained, in the black sheet.

"That will be all," the commanding voice says to Nora.

She turns to leave. "Charming child. I look forward to knowing her better."

Both of their voices carry a trace of the South. Not Texas, but . . .

I force out the questions because I need to hear the answers. "Where am I? What have you done to me?"

"I've taken care of you, made sure your elevation was as protected as it could be. Sugar, you've been spared the spiraling moods, the paranoia and indignity, the cramps and shooting pain. The erratic and unpredictable behavior. Tonight your month-long transformation is behind us." He leads me to a window, pulls back the drapes. It's open, but the icy wind is no bother. "Tonight the world is ours."

Below, a crowd has gathered in the moonlight. Hundreds of jovial bodies, perhaps as many as a thousand, swirling, bobbing. They're the dead of winter, and they're dancing in the falling snow. Wind ravages their flowing hair, tosses up their capes and full-length skirts, spreads their draping sleeves like rodent wings. Against the white of the landscape, they swirl in black and red, in gray and violet.

Surveying the scene, I can almost count their eyelashes, the needles of the evergreens. The revelers sing my name: "Miranda!"

"I've turned you into a princess," he explains, "and you're a pretty one at that. These folks are our aristocracy. They've come together to celebrate."

A princess. Images from movies and storybooks flit through my mind—ball gowns and poison apples and beauties awakened with a kiss ... dark magic and evil wizards and knights on white horses, riding to the rescue. I search the crowd below for someone, anyone trying to save me. If only it wasn't so hard to concentrate. "Thirsty."

"Let's do something about that." He waves, and the crowd shrieks with glee at the sight of us together.

Master, he called himself. Majesty. Father. Still wrapped in the black sheet, I mimic his actions, the royal wave. I know only one word. "Yes."

Newly appareled in an off-the-shoulder charcoal gown, I twist in the front passenger seat of the black Caddy to study my immense new home. The multilevel white stone building is set deep on the property, far from the road. The red tower roofs look like pointy hats. A red dragon on a black flag ripples in the wind. It's a castle.

"Fancy, isn't it?" Father asks from behind the wheel. "We have nine more like it and another being built right now. This here is our U.S. Midwest regional estate. Like all the rest, it's loosely inspired by Castle Bran in Transylvania (or so I like to tell folks). It's quite the fortress, too—the back wall is eleven feet thick."

We wait for the wrought-iron gate to open. It reminds me of the gate at the cemetery, only this one is well oiled and freshly painted black. "What's that?"

A large canine circles the car. It's a shepherd—no, a wolf, the size of a Great Dane, his eyes blood bright. They capture and deaden, not that it matters. I'm beyond their power. The wolflike creature bows its head, tucks its tail, and whines.

"Sentry," Father explains. "We have six prowling the grounds."

I stretch my arms forward, feeling the power pulse through me. If I wanted to, I could rip this car apart. "They're like us?"

"No one is like us, sugar plum, but they are eternals."

Eternals. The way he says it, it sounds like *gods.*

I try to imagine myself changing into the shape of a wolf. It's such a silly thought. I take another sip from the straw to stop myself from giggling.

On our stroll from my bedroom through the castle to the parking garage, Father offered me a drink from a crystal decanter, and I told him I wasn't twenty-one. He said that no longer mattered. He reminded me that, in a way, I won't be getting any older. That's a silly thought, too.

Faintly, I realize it's not alcohol that's making me drunk.

"The castle," Father continues, "sits at the highest point of Whitby Estates. It's the most moneyed community on Chicago's North Shore. Many of our favored aristocracy own and occupy the homes hereabouts."

In my fuzzy state, it takes me a moment to sift

through to the part that makes the least sense. "We're not in Dallas?"

His smile is toothy. "Sip your blood wine."

I do. I listen, intent, as Father turns the radio to a country music station and explains my faux pas with Nora, the castle chef. He says there is human property useful for work (as she is) or for companionship and entertainment, like pets. Like my pet gerbil, I think. The rest are merely food.

"We drink their blood," he adds, steering through the stately neighborhood, "and sometimes toy with their bodies. We don't eat their flesh, though. That's the nasty business of shifters."

My first trip to the city! It's big; it's brash. It's a bloody blur.

Father shows off, taking more than he needs. In the loop de loop (Father says it's just called the Loop), he tells me that the investment banker tastes of vodka. Later, at the blues club across town, he mocks the fading beat of a drummer's heart.

Within the next hour, Father drops a drained runaway teenager (her bus ticket read *Iowa City*) into a nearby alley and asks, "Thirsty, sugar?"

I sway, my hands clasped behind my back. It's all I

can do not to drop and suckle from the discarded girl's wound. "Yes, Father," I say. "Yes, yes, yes."

Our next stop is Greek Town, and, shoving a waiter against a brick wall, I hardly glimpse his face. I'm someplace else, diving into dark liquid, luxuriating in an endless sea, warm for the first time tonight. It's bliss . . . the thick, sweet taste, the scent of blood and lamb and unfamiliar spices.

Teetering on tiptoe, I realize there's an easier way. I snap the neck for a better angle, and, still nursing the vein, move the waiter into a kneeling position. It's better, *much* better, yes.

Lapping at a stray trickle, I'm only vaguely aware of Father speaking into his cell phone. He whispers of the victims we've left behind.

Missing Miranda

A YEAR LOST

It's been a year tonight since the last time I saw
Miranda.

I was home from UNT last weekend for my little brother's birthday, and I spotted Miranda's mom at the fish
counter at Whole Foods. She was buying shrimp and
scallops. I was picking up some crab dip because my
grandparents were coming over.

I was kind of scared to say hi. Miz Shen didn't talk
to me last spring at the candlelight vigil. I think she
blamed me for what happened. That's okay. I blamed
me, too.

But when she saw me, she gave me this huge hug and
started crying right there in the grocery store. Her mas-
cara ran down her face in tiny black streams. She didn't
care how she looked or what anyone thought. I didn't
either. I started crying, too.

The resident assistant at my dorm keeps telling me, "It's not all on your shoulders."

I know. I know I'm not the only one who cares. I'm probably not even the best person to help.

If the guy I met that night, the good guy, is reading this, please *write*. At least that way I won't be worried about both of you.

Comments Link

Miranda

IT'S BEEN TWELVE AND A HALF MONTHS since I first awakened in this castle.

I minimize the Eternal News Network (ENN) website on my browser, amused by the streaming coverage of tonight's event. I'm not nervous, not really.

As early as my first hunt with Father, I've made a positive impression. Songs are still sung in praise of that night, odes recited.

It's true that I was off-balance for a while, struck down by soul sickness—the tedious burdens of guilt and despair—immediately afterward and for the first few months that followed. But, fortunately, that foolishness has faded with time.

I skip to an arched window of the pink-and-black suite, unofficially called the nursery, and wave to subjects arriving via the red carpet. Cameras flash, and jewels sparkle. I'm finally the life of the party. All I had to do was die.

Lucy would say, Enough with the drama queen.

I almost wish she were here. Who better to confide in than my vampire fan girl/best friend? Make that eternal aficionado/most treasured companion.

Did that make sense? I'm not sure, but I've been making a determined effort. Father objects to the V-word and insists we speak formally, especially when around company. It's all about maintaining appearances. I practice constantly, even in my head, so I don't slip up.

Oh, how Father loves to entertain! For my demonic debut, he's summoned the glittering, gossipy aristocracy to the castle's largest, and central, interior courtyard.

The night is lit with torches, punctuated by round tables strung with dewy white lilies and roses. The reflecting pool has been hidden behind shimmering silver curtains.

It's April first, a fool's night. No one who matters minds the cold.

The cuisine is nouveau-Romanian-meets-southern-fried. It's available mostly for the consumption of the decked-out personal assistants (at events like this, they're as much fashion accessories as they are helpmates).

The majority of our more-honored guests are on an all-liquid diet. For that, humans from the castle's stock—gagged, blindfolded, and bound—have been affixed to the surrounding white rock walls. Boys and girls, young and tasty, runaways mostly. If they run dry, we have more in the dungeon.

And then there are those candidates for pleasures beyond drinking. They're scrubbed cleaner. Their light-blue hospital gowns have been replaced with sheer lavender robes that match the linen napkins and tablecloths.

In a few minutes, they'll be offered as party favors, and the guest rooms will be opened to those who prefer to indulge their peccadilloes in private.

The party has raged since an hour after sunset, as is traditional—the hour to provide travel and setup time. We can tolerate daylight, but it weakens us and Father despises weakness.

He waves an empty crystal glass, and his personal assistant (PA) refills it with blood wine. They exchange a meaningful look, and then the PA, Harrison, checks the diamond-rimmed face of his Rolex, a Solstice bonus for outstanding service.

I've come to rely on Harrison myself. He's an elegant

man—slender, sexy, and always impeccably dressed. At age forty, with great bone structure and better skin, he's a rather youthful Alfred to Father's Batman, or so he fancies himself.

We didn't get off to the best of starts, Harrison and me. He was brusque, I was flailing, and I don't think he appreciated having to compete for Father's attention.

Nora says he's simply suspicious of newcomers. It's something about his childhood and lingering issues with trust. That makes a certain sense.

Harrison is one of those legacy servants who come so highly prized, the latest of a five-generation line. Still, he and his brother might never have survived if their original mistress, Penelope—she lives in the bungaloid mansion across the street—hadn't found their resemblance to each other amusing.

I can't imagine what it must have been like for Harrison as a human child growing up in this world. I like him, though, and at this point, I think he likes me, too. It's simply as if we've mutually decided not to admit it aloud.

Tonight has been a long, chilly one, largely spent making small talk, cooing over the string trio, complimenting fashions ranging from the smashing to the questionable to the clichéd. This is my formal introduction to society, my first public event of any significant scale, and Father is giving me more leash than I expected.

Every time I turn around, I'm fawned over by another guest.

"Delightful gala, princess!"

"A magnificent occasion!"

"Love your dress!"

Sometimes I pause to chat. Usually, I offer only the slightest nod of acknowledgment. Father told me earlier to respond at my discretion.

Worldwide, the aristocracy numbers in the thousands, which of course the courtyard couldn't accommodate. Consequently, the guest list is limited to a preferred hundred or so, most in the company of their PAs.

To my knowledge, the only Old Blood invited tonight is the infamous Sabine from Paris. So far, her arrival hasn't been announced. I look forward to meeting her and finding out what all the fuss is about.

Unlike his predecessors, Father tends to socially slight Old Bloods, possibly because they make him uncomfortable and probably because they constitute a threat.

I'm not sure of the political wisdom of his strategy. However, Father defeated an Old Blood predecessor to claim the Mantle. "We must develop our supernatural talents," he once told me, "but daring, scheming, and opportunism can trump raw ability."

He should know. Father is The Dracula himself (not that anyone calls him that around the house). The current Dracula, not the original of course. Nevertheless, the reigning exalted master of eternals.

He's not only powerful for his age; he also has abilities beyond his years. I did some research. An anonymous source told the *Eternal Herald-Gazette* that this was the result of his dabbling in unstable magic—that the price of those spells could prove to be his sanity itself. I don't know if that's true, but if so, it explains his unpredictability.

I wander to join the A-list conversation.

Father raises his glass to the latest news from the Middle East. "Our numbers are up there," he gloats. "Perhaps we should stir the conflict again."

Many eternals are elevated on the battlefield, as Father himself was. He, despite sometimes affecting a Romanian accent, was born an American and blessed with unholy blood at Fredericksburg, Virginia, during the Civil War. Tonight he's speaking in his pseudo-European "company" voice. The one he uses to impress.

As a native Texan, I privately think it's a shame he's embarrassed by his slight southern accent. However, the aristocracy is influential, prone to stereotyping and utter snobbishness.

"Ah, sugar plum," Father greets me. "How kind of you to join us! I've given this party in your honor, and I've hardly seen you all night."

"Please forgive me." I feel a flash of panic. I thought I was supposed to circulate. Father doesn't sound angry, though. Perhaps this time he's merely teasing. "It's only that your inner circle is so refined. I'm the only teenage eternal present." Although a number in attendance could pass for one. "And . . ."

My mind goes blank. I hoped to flatter my way out, but I have no idea how to pull it off. I didn't grow up around this kind of crowd. Despite Father's best efforts to train me, I'm still seriously out of my element.

"We old fogies aren't doing it for you?" asks Elina, in a red sheath with matching spiked heels. She's all curves and curls, more lush than I am, more woman-shaped. She has painted-on eyebrows, and she's forked her tongue with a pair of pinking shears.

I wonder how old she is, how powerful. Father presented me with profiles of all the guests to study a few nights ago, but her age wasn't in her file.

Elina's consort Victor bends to kiss my hand. "Charmed to meet you, Your Highness." He's lithe, but mean and well muscled. There's a necklace of human baby teeth around his neck.

So far tonight, Elina and Victor are the most normal couple I've met.

"Were you criticizing my beloved child?" Father asks her.

At first, Elina shrinks at the suggestion. "No, sire."

Then she regains her bravado as Victor caresses her bare back. "I was simply trying to draw the girl out."

Father's fangs descend. "Perhaps this will help."

At the snap of Father's fingers, Harrison sets the bottle of blood wine on a passing waiter's tray; rushes to the middle of the courtyard; and draws back the full-length, silver curtains, revealing a youthful male figure bound on a platform.

That accomplished, the PA strolls through the crowd, ringing a small bell to announce the show.

"Now?" Elina asks.

"Now," Father replies.

In a puff of smoke and shadows, she transforms from woman to bat.

Older. She's older and more formidable than I thought. An Old Blood.

Elina careens toward tonight's sacrifice and rips off his hood with her claws.

Flint, formerly one of Father's enforcers, strains against the chains. He . . . no, not he—*it*. The condemned are unworthy of a gender pronoun.

In bat form, Elina circles it once, and then the gag is gone, too.

Sometimes Father enjoys the silence.

Sometimes he prefers to hear them scream.

"No, master, please," pleads the mewling thing. "I'll be good, I promise."

I wondered why the curtains were positioned like that, who was to be executed.

Normally, the reflecting pool looks innocuous. Now, though, the dunking platform, triggering target, and heavy iron chains have been released from a curved steel wall that has been rolled into place and locked around it.

"Always remember that you are royalty. You defer to no one but me." Father hands me a baseball. "Take this."

I consider the condemned. I don't know how it fell short. Yet those who refuse to apply for hunting licenses, to pay taxes on their victims, to hunt with discretion, to treat aristocracy and, most important, royalty with respect are to be extinguished. That's usually the enforcers' responsibility. Tonight, it's my pleasure.

"Anytime you're ready," Father says, and I suppress the sudden memory of Ms. Esposito calling the same words to me on my high-school stage.

Father loves the dunking platform. It's his brain-child, his game. A spray of holy water burns like acid, but submersion creates a visual feast as the body evaporates on contact with an impressive *whoosh* noise—a crowd pleaser.

It's something I admire about Father, his sense of theater.

My midnight gray taffeta gown is tight through the shoulders. If I'd known what he had been planning, I would've chosen something more maneuverable.

"Miranda?" Father clears his throat. "Sugar?"

I tuck the baseball under my arm and remove the black-pearl-and-platinum bracelet Father gave me (along with the car) earlier tonight. Harrison's gloved hand extends to take it for safekeeping.

I weigh the ball in my hand. It's from the 1908 World Series.

Father is a devoted Cubs fan.

"Something wrong?" he asks.

I shake my head, mindful of our audience. Our favored wait with rapt attention.

I gaze one last time at Flint. He has a broad chest, a mane of blond hair, and pink, bowed lips that have gone white from starvation.

It can't have been easy for him these past few weeks in the dungeon, separated from our bleeding stock by stone and bars.

The condemned protests again. "Princess, no!" He, *it*, strains against the chains, not much older than me, too new to escape by changing form. "No!"

I toss the ball. Catch it. In life, I wasn't especially athletic, but I've always had good hand-eye coordination.

"Miranda!" it pleads again. "Miranda!"

I can feel Father's impatience as he crosses his arms in custom formalwear.

Falling snow reflects the moonlight. It smells so fresh, so clean.

"Ten, nine," the crowd mutters. "Eight." Their voices rise. "Seven."

The countdown goes on, louder and louder.

At "one," I haul off and pitch the ball.

Bull's-eye. *Whoosh.*

I've never before killed one of my own kind. I lick my lips, satisfied.

"Nicely done," Father growls in my ear.

I'm triumphant, resplendent by his side. Our subjects swirl around us—prancing, dancing, swooping, and howling. Living party favors in clawed hands, blood streaming from greedy mouths. We are the calm at the center of their storm.

I fold my hands in front of my waist, prim and demure, feeling utterly comfortable in my skin, however cold it may be.

Our guests throw back their heads and roar through their teeth, "Hail Miranda!"

Miranda

THREE NIGHTS AFTER MY PARTY, Harrison delivers a thin girl with smudges beneath her eyes to my bedroom suite. Her blue tunic does little to hide her emaciated physique or the tracks on her arms. She can't be more than fifteen.

"Mistress," Harrison begins, "the master's teleconference with the Brazilians has run longer than expected. He's still downstairs in the east-wing meeting room." The PA shoves the girl to the floor, and when she raises her head, she's crying.

"Thank you," I say. "That will be all."

"Very good," Harrison replies. He shuts the arched door behind him, and, with my heightened hearing, I note that his retreating footsteps are brisk down the hall.

Early on, when I was plagued by soul sickness, it shocked me that our staff could offer up fellow humans the way they do. I'm no longer inclined to dwell on the matter, but I still don't understand how they live with themselves.

The openly sobbing girl here tonight is tall with long legs and long blond hair. She's thinner, with less muscle and spark, and yet she reminds me of Lucy. Or at least what Lucy might've been if she were poor and abused.

I want the girl to be quiet. I want to pluck out her eyes—hazel eyes like Lucy's—and suck them dry. But I can't. Not this time. Not this girl.

I cross to the antique cherry desk and tap a button on the phone. "Nora?"

"What can I do for you, honey?" the chef replies.

"I'll pass on dinner tonight. Could someone clear her out of my room?"

The hesitation lasts longer than it should. "Did the offering displease you?"

I consider the possibility that the resemblance between Lucy and my dinner isn't a coincidence, that it's a test. A test from heaven or a test from hell. It has to be hell, though, doesn't it? Father is fond of his games, and there's nothing holy here.

I take a risk and admit the truth. "No," I say. "I've lost my appetite."

THE OFFICE OF
THE ARCHANGEL MICHAEL
The Sword of Heaven
The Bringer of Souls

To: Joshua
From: Michael
Date: Saturday, April 5

Our sympathies on the loss of your latest assignment and his camel. Rest assured that they have been joyfully reunited in the Pearly Gates Lobby Lounge.

Until further notice, you are directed to conduct studious observation of the following two individuals: the angel Zachary and the vampire Miranda.

Complete and file A-127B forms on both subjects by midnight CST April 12.
See attached Yahoo! maps.

Miranda

THOUGH WE ETERNALS AREN'T REQUIRED to sleep in coffins, Father insists on it. I don't mind. Mine is a top-of-the-line cherry and mahogany number with platinum fittings and a well-padded, pearl-velvet interior. We saved seventy percent by ordering online.

My luxury box is a demure complement to Father's. His is king-size and made from black marble, customized with brass fittings and a NASCAR emblem. It could be fairly characterized as the black-velvet Elvis painting of coffins.

They're arranged side by side in the fully stocked wine cellar.

It's a large circular room with fourteen-foot ceilings, masculine in its dark woods, barrel-based tables, leather club chairs, and humidor. The collection of reds numbers well over two thousand, the rarest and finest of dust-covered labels.

There are four doors, one leading to the stairs, two leading (respectively) to my private bath and to Father's, and the last one opening to the dungeon, for those occasions when someone wants to create a blood-wine blend.

As of this week, my official time in the third-floor nursery is over. I have conquered my soul sickness. I have embraced my new existence. Father has declared my neophyte status behind us and now considers me a full-fledged eternal.

It's strange. I used to fantasize about being an actress, in the spotlight as the crowd tossed long-stemmed roses at my feet. The one time I went for it was a disaster.

Now that I'm dead, it's like every night is opening night, all of it is improv, and I'm a superstar (with no experience).

"Something wrong, sugar?" Father asks. "You're not drinking from the vein of late." His voice echoes in the room, slides under my skin, and festers.

The suddenness of the inquiry takes me off-guard, though I know he's been paying attention. Ever since I turned away the not-Lucy girl. . . . That was the Friday before last, and I still can't stop thinking about her.

I make my way out of my box. "I, well, it's not that I'm being all—"

"Language, sugar plum. Believe in yourself." He says

that in a supportive and understanding way, but sometimes when my princess persona falters, the South rises in
his voice and his eyes flash red.

I compose myself. "I prefer my blood, my blood wine, by
the glass." I smooth my sleeping gown. "My clothes are so
nice." No, that won't do. "Forgive me, I meant to say, I adore
having such lovely apparel. I fret staining the material."

Like much of the castle, the dim cellar is lit only by the
candelabra, making it harder to decipher Father's expression. He shakes his head. "Forgive me for not making
myself clear on the matter. You're welcome to wear your
garments once and toss them to the maids to be used as
rags. We can always commission more."

I'm relieved by his response and, even after all this
time, amazed by our infinite budget. My human parents
were solidly middle-class, but unless the outfit was for a
special occasion, my mom bought most of my new clothes
on sale.

Father paces a moment. "Although now that you mention it, why indeed should a crown princess be expected to
sully herself? Forgive me for not realizing. Leiko was one
of your people, and she never could tolerate a smudge or
pulled thread. Your dining preferences are up to you, so
long as you're well fed."

I have no idea who Leiko is or was, but the name
sounds Japanese.

I'm Chinese American on Mom's side, Scottish

American on Dad's. I've mentioned my heritage in passing to Father only once or twice.

I decide it's best to ignore the "your people" reference. In his day, it was probably considered polite (or at least that's what I tell myself).

Father pauses and gives me a meaningful look. "Still, we must be mindful of your image. We wouldn't want anyone thinking your cleanly ways are getting in the way of your true nature."

By "anyone," he's referring to eternal society. Beyond us, it's composed of the aristocracy, gentry, and lesser subjects (sentries, enforcers, those who have to rent). Rogues skirt the periphery, for as long as they last anyway. Defiance equals suicide.

He gives me a quick kiss on the forehead. "Come to think of it, now that you have an understanding of your station, you might as well choose your own clothing."

I must admit a particular thrill at that. In life, shopping for clothes was this ongoing negotiation with my mom. She pushed for me to dress the way she did, like the former beauty queen she was. I felt more comfortable in petite versions of whatever Lucy liked. Oversize T-shirts and jeans or thrift-store finds.

Now, everything is different. Last week, a photographer shot me wrapped only in a sheer, long, sparkly crimson scarf for the cover of *Eternal Elegance* magazine. If I had more blood in my system, I'd still be blushing.

When I first arrived, the clothes that filled the wardrobe upstairs were regular size tens instead of my usual petite fours or sixes. Father corrected that in a hurry, assuring me that Italy's most *magnifico* designer was sketching until her fingers bled and then sketching with her own blood. More gowns arrive each day. And because of a few subtle words from Nora about "my adjustment" to eternal life, I also have casual clothes, if you can call a thousand-dollar, hand-stitched T-shirt "casual."

What I like best about being a princess is having maids. I used to hate to clean my room. I did it; don't get me wrong. I wasn't some hopeless slob, and anyway, my mom would've grounded me if I didn't straighten up. Yet to say it wasn't a pleasure is an understatement.

Our maids, Katerina, Lisa, Charlotte, and Renée, attend to the needs of the castle, its sovereigns, and the rest of our staff. They're all related, sisters or cousins. Each is willowy, with pale skin and light pink eyes. Nora mentioned that one of their grandmothers was an albino. I'd be interested to know more, but Father explained that there is a hierarchy to one's servants. Maids rank no better than gardeners. They are to be spoken to, but not personally or at any length.

Among other duties, they clean, maintain the candles,

wash the linens, run household errands, restock the toiletries, and deliver food to and from the dungeon.

Renée and Charlotte—at least I think they're Renée and Charlotte—are with me now. At the moment, I'm trying on the latest additions to my wardrobe in what was once my nursery but recently I've begun to think of as my retreat.

"How's it coming?" I ask.

"Forgive our clumsiness, Your Highness," one murmurs. "The buttons are small, and our fingers are large and fumbling."

The maids are fastening me into a rare black vintage gown (it involves a hoop, a corset, and a padded push-up bra). With each button, I feel more like a refugee from the prom of the damned. Yet it's the sort of thing Father adores, and he is my underworld.

The dress must be assembled in three sections along the back, each with a row of one hundred black pearl buttons. More skim from my ruffled black lace cuffs, up the length of my forearms. The neckline extends to midshoulder, and the skirt falls in ruffled tiers. The black knit hose sent to accompany the ensemble are thigh-high and fasten to a garter belt. I'd never be able to manage all this without help.

The other maid maneuvers a freestanding full-length oval mirror in front of me. "We've got it now," she says, "for your approval."

My reflection is faded, translucent. It doesn't matter. I'm exquisite. I don't mean that to sound conceited. In life, I never thought of myself as a remarkable-looking girl. Yet, as an eternal, I'm not only transformed; I'm *transformed.* My skin glows, fairer than before. The blue of my eyes has lost intensity, but that only makes me want to look deeper, to see what's there. My hair is longer, shinier, though that could be from the maids' weekly deep-conditioning treatment, a service I never had while alive.

"Your Highness," the maids say. They mean me.

"Sugar," Father begins, "it takes effort and patience and"—he leans in close at my right—"occasional regurgitation to build up to eating solid food. Most eternals don't bother. They stick to liquids."

Nora sets a sea-green rectangular plate topped with a sliced asparagus tempura roll in front of us. It's the latest of several vegetarian sushi dishes, each garnished with ginger, wasabi, and thread-cut radish.

We're in the kitchen, seated on tall metal stools at the bar sink counter. Though the castle as a whole is a juxtaposition of the contemporary and historical, this room reeks of twenty-first-century conveniences.

I feel Father watching me raise the smooth black chopsticks. Asian heritage aside, I've never gotten the hang . . . I mean, my mastery of the devices has been lacking. I make an effort to position them the way Mom showed me time and again.

"I do miss food I can chew," I say, not for the first time.

My first attempt results in my flinging a piece of the roll onto the tile.

Nora hands me a set of wooden chopsticks engraved with dragon heads. They're less slippery, and on my third try I manage to slide some sushi into my mouth.

I can tell Father is unimpressed, but I don't expect him to say: "Sugar, I hate to have to tell you this, but I have bad news."

"News?" I ask, forcing myself to swallow, covering my mouth with the green linen napkin when the food threatens to come back up.

"Harrison informs me," he begins, "that the maids are questioning your strength. They're saying you've still got too much soul in you." He shrugs. "Servants do prattle on. It was the same when I was a human, though we called them 'slaves' back then. Their tongues wag."

I thought the maids were on my side! Annoyed, I mutter, "Why do they need tongues, anyway?"

With his chopsticks, Father stirs wasabi into his soy sauce. "Why, indeed?"

He excuses himself, leaving the room without an explanation. For a while, Nora keeps me company, and before I know it, Father is seated at my side once again.

Harrison joins us in the kitchen moments later, and

it's Nora's expression upon seeing the silver tray he carries that catches my eye. She's aghast.

I turn my attention to what's being displayed—four pieces of meat.

"What's that?" I ask.

"Maid's tongue," Father replies, "like you suggested. Four maids' tongues, to be precise." He gestures with his sticks. His voice is merry. "Would you care to partake?"

I fight the urge to recoil, realizing it's another test. "No, thank you," I say. "We don't eat human flesh. That is the nasty business of shifters."

I'm pleased with my answer. It's taken almost verbatim from Father's explanation of it to me on my first night in the black Caddy and at least twice since.

Without warning, Father shoves our plates off the counter and tosses the bowls across the room, creating a cacophony of small crashes. "Are you back-talkin' me?"

"No!" I'm on my feet, not caring as a piece of ceramic cuts through my feathered, red house slipper. "No, Father, of course not."

I've seen his fangs before, in the hunt—not bared against me.

Harrison has abandoned the tray and cleared the room.

Nora has ducked behind the counter.

Father curls his clawed hands, as if to strike.

"I'm sorry!" I exclaim, bewildered. "Daddy, please! I apologize."

A fist lashes toward my face with enough power behind it to punch a hole through my skull, only to dissolve into smoke a breath before contact. Father's physical form, now a swirl of dark, putrid air, twists and rages before exiting beneath the kitchen door.

I'm not breathing heavily, only because I don't have to breathe. My heart isn't beating rapidly, only because it doesn't beat at all. "What just happened?" I exclaim. "Nora, what did I do wrong?"

She stands from behind the counter, her gaze never leaving the doorway. "You couldn't win, hon. He's angry that you turned down what he offered and, worse, that you dared to correct him."

"But I thought —"

"I know, I know. The fact of the matter is, he probably would've hollered at you just as bad if you'd broken his rules and took the bait. Maybe worse."

"That's totally unfair!" I say. "It doesn't even make sense."

"The master is powerful for his age," she replies, wiping her hands on her apron. "More powerful, it seems, with each passing night."

It's the magic, I realize. The rumors must be true. Father *is* using spells to become more powerful. And it's costing him his sanity.

Miranda

SERVANTS AND SENTRIES ASIDE, on a night-to-night basis, it's only the two of us.

Tonight Father explained why. Over the past century, all three of his brides were taken from him—Giselle by self-proclaimed "vampire hunters" who staked her after a performance of the Vienna State Opera in the 1930s; Leiko, whose own cigarette, I've recently learned, set her coffin on fire aboard our yacht off the coast of Crete in the 1970s; and Yolanda, whose head and limbs were torn off by rogues at a rodeo in Albuquerque two years ago.

"I'm not taking any chances with you, sugar," he concluded. "No chances at all."

We spend most of our early evenings in the torch-lit parlor. (I suspect an Eastern European Dracula, or for that matter most castle dwellers, would refer to it as "the main hall," but here Father's preferences rule.) I sip blood wine, he sips blood-and-mint juleps, and we discuss matters of state. Later, he puffs on his Cuban cigars, and I study *The Blood Drinker's Guide*. It's available on CD-ROM, but something about turning the musty yellow pages is soothing.

Perhaps that sounds anticlimactic. Lucy would call much of our eternal lifestyle a bore, and arguably, compared to Hollywood's misrepresentations, it is.

Yet eternals keep a low profile. Our existence isn't a secret. The humans' prevailing theory, though, is that we're few, solitary, and can order blood online (true, though there are quality-control issues) rather than hunt the unsuspecting.

Some know better—those in certain cities, certain walks of life. Bartenders, cabbies, hairstylists, doormen— the people who know everything, they're aware of our greater presence. They also know enough to stay quiet and stay away.

Worldwide law enforcement and militaries are more complicated. We have something of an understanding about who's fair game and who isn't. They pay in blood if they violate our space. We pay in cash if we violate theirs. But even within approved hunting zones, valued members of human society—especially children, clergy, and anyone in a uniform—are supposed to be off the menu. For the most part, we hold to that.

A small percentage of their kind can't be touched at all, politically speaking—hence the controversy around that incident in Dallas.

The irony? It wasn't one of us that the witness spotted. The whole conspiracy theory sprang out of a very mundane and mortal case of pinkeye. Still, the story keeps the prey wary and their media alert, neither of which is in our global best interests.

Speaking of global, Father is about to take his much-belated annual world tour, which will include stops in New York, London, Munich, Moscow, Sydney, Tokyo, Jakarta, Rio, Johannesburg, and Cairo. Last spring's tour was canceled after Father announced himself on paternity leave from public appearances. Consequently, the anticipation surrounding this upcoming trip is higher than ever. I'm not sure why he isn't taking me along. I do know better, though, than to ask.

"After I've wrapped up the routine business," he begins, "I'm going to . . ." He raises the cigar to his lips and kicks out the footrest of his La-Z-Boy.

Torch lighting aside, most of the castle furnishings reflect the Arts-and-Crafts and prairie styles that characterize the neighborhood. That's the baseline. It's liberally augmented by an eclectic array of treasures, mounted animal heads, leather-bound books, and acquisitions from international travels.

The knives that Father collects are displayed in more rooms than not, some in lead-paned cases, others artfully set on shelves. We have two that Jack the Ripper presented to him last year, and Father checks every night for additional acquisitions via his merchant contacts and eBay.

The European dragon theme borders on exhausting. Dragon-foot designs can be found on bathtubs, bookends, candlesticks, and urns. A dragon also graces our crest, which appears on numerous tapestries as well as on our flags, wine labels, linens, coasters, and souvenir mugs. It's the symbol of the Mantle of Dracul and, consequently, it's everywhere. Father frequently points it out, and I make appropriate cooing noises.

He doesn't talk about the horse bronzes or the oil paintings of Virginia landscapes, though, most notably the one labeled *Radford Plantation*.

"Harrison!" Father calls, setting his cigar on a brass tray table.

"Master?" The PA sniffs appreciatively. He's been known to pinch from the master's humidor in the cellar.

"You'll watch over the household staff while I'm on the road, won't you?" Father reaches over, touches Harrison's forearm. "I won't be long."

A month to the date. That would be May 14.

Harrison's returning smile is a knowing one. "Of course."

"It's time our princess of darkness hired her own PA," Father adds. "You have enough to do without catering to my baby girl, don't you?"

I'm intrigued by the idea of having my own PA. It's such a grown-up status symbol, not that all of us embrace the old tradition. In today's world of security systems, pizza delivery and dry cleaning, one-night stands and Internet shopping, many find personal assistants passé. Yet I look forward to having someone report to me first.

"Of course," Harrison agrees again. Not that disagreeing is an option.

"Jim-dandy!" Father concludes. "That reminds me. Be a good man and call the executive temp service in New York. I'll still need my own PA while I'm abroad."

Translation: Harrison is replaceable, if only in the short term.

He's too savvy to offer anything but a final "of course" and exit the parlor. Yet I hear him mutter, "Be a good man" in a mocking way as he fades from view.

At least the castle will be less lonely with Harrison around.

Father shifts his attention to me. "Sugar, I'll be counting on you to maintain order and oversee the management of this estate. Not to fret, Harrison will mind the details.

We royals aren't hands-on, after all. Just be available in case he needs the guiding hand of a superior being."

A superior being. I like the sound of that. I set down *The Blood Drinker's Guide* and cross my legs, clothed in silk pajamas, on the worn werebear rug in front of the crackling fireplace. The color of the silk matches my skin, suggesting a nude or a ghost. It makes my dark hair and blue eyes more striking, I hope. It's exhausting being precious all the time.

Father is fairly impressive himself. He has a mesmerizing voice—no matter how he elects to use it—a killer smile, and looks to be in his midfifties, though in truth it's not too early to start thinking about his bicentennial.

"While I'm gone," he goes on, "Harrison will keep me informed of any unsavory developments. And you, sugar plum, shall busy yourself with choosing your PA and"— Father beams at me—"planning my gala."

I'm stunned. For our kind, Father's deathday is an international holiday rivaling Halloween. He schedules the celebration on a whim each spring, depending on his mood and the weather. In-the-know invitees arrive in the Chicago area early, poised to pounce and party. The pressure is on. Like his tour, last year's was canceled.

This is the first time I've been given a responsibility beyond looking beautiful and making socially appropriate conversation. It's as flattering as it is nerve-racking.

"Yes, Father," I reply. "Thank you."

I'm his only daughter, his only child. Yet it wouldn't be hard for him to "adopt" another. It was only last night that he threatened me in the kitchen. Tonight we appear to be pretending it never happened.

I glance at the portrait of Father and his three brides, hanging over the fireplace mantle, at Yolanda, who was torn to pieces. He could rip off my head if he wanted to.

"Take care, sugar," he says. "I'll be seeing you."

Before I can muster up a suitable reply, Father has already dissolved into mist. He can't make it to New York that way, but the detached garage is easy enough.

Eternal Herald-Gazette

Tuesday, April 15

================= **CLASSIFIED ADS** =================

Wanted: Personal assistant to Her Royal Highness. Duties: Whatever is asked, without hesitation, including but not limited to secretarial/administrative, household, defense, blood donation, driving, companionship, prey disposal, and love slavery. Required: Athleticism, high school diploma (3.25 GPA or better), discretion. Preferred: Age 17–25, human. Salary based on experience and pedigree. Standard executive-staff benefits apply. See the eternal governmental website for PDF application and additional information.

Zachary

I WAKE UP IN THE DARK on a cushioned slab, rolling side-ways. I fall fast. Land hard with a thud, hitting the floor and a wall. My head is throbbing. My shoulder's sore. I'm barefoot, and I'm sweating in a white-and-lime-colored poncho I don't recognize. Beneath it, I have on a white T and a faded pair of burnt-orange sweatpants.

Is this a morgue? Am I dead? *Can* I die? Before, that was impossible. But now?

I push damp curls from my forehead. The room is moving, clacking, and swaying.

A train. Where is it? Where's it going? How did I get on board?

As I sit up, my stomach heaves. I haul myself to my feet, look out the window at a pasture dotted with cows, and check the empty combination toilet-shower.

I think back on last night. My latest "landlord" tossing me out of her futon and her apartment in Austin's French Place neighborhood. She was tired of hearing me mumble Miranda's name in my sleep.

I caught a ride with a neighbor to South Congress. Used the last of my cash to buy a flight or three of tequila.

Later, I was nearly mowed down by a cute redhead in a long yellow convertible when I stepped into the crosswalk from behind a SUV. Somebody—beats me who—pulled me back to safety. After that, I must've blacked out.

I open my mouth. Curl my fuzzy tongue. That's when it hits me—the mysterious savior, the lost time, the miraculous train ticket. This is a private room, to boot.

A human might call it lucky. A human might chalk it up to Fate. Or enroll in Alcoholics Anonymous. But I'm not a human. I never have been.

Am I an *assignment*? Or is this a onetime bailout? "Who's there?"

No luck.

I look to the ceiling. "Come on," I say. "Fess up."

Still nothing.

"Hey! Joshua? Nick? Jamilya? Is that you?"

The possibilities are in the billions. But it figures that one of my closer buds would be sent. "Um, Aaron? Deb?

Maria? Farid? Natalie? If you're listening, I could use a bottle of water, a shower, a shave, fresh clothes, and a clue."

"You don't ask for much, do you?" comes the answer from thin air.

Hang on, not from thin air. I slide the door open and stumble into the hall.

"Hello, earth angel!" he exclaims. It's my best friend, Joshua. His wings are folded. He's grinning like a fool.

Josh tosses a bright blue canvas bag into my cabin and pulls me into a bear hug. "Man, I've missed you!" Then he moves back. Josh makes a show of holding his nose and waving his hand in front of it. "Whew. Somebody's ripe. Take a hint, doofus! You got the room with a shower for a reason."

"I, you . . ." It's been fourteen months since I last saw him. Long enough that I've been starting to wonder if I'm crazy. If my memories are real or delusions. How I threw away so much so fast. "What are you doing here?"

Josh's voice goes flat. "Gabriel says hi."

Gabriel. An archangel, like Michael (The Sword of Heaven, The Bringer of Souls, also known as He Who Booted Me).

Between my hangover and homesickness, it's past time to change the subject. "Not that I'm not glad to see you. But why are you here again?"

He shrugs. "I've been watching you for a while."

I keep my voice casual. "Spying on me, you mean?"

That's embarrassing. At first, I did okay in Dallas. After failing to turn up any more leads on Kurt or Miranda, I volunteered at a youth shelter for about eight months and spent most of my nights there. But I couldn't save them all. After I met a girl who looked too much like Miranda, I gave it up. The way I saw it, sooner or later, I was going to hell anyway. If you had to be homeless and damned, the weather and politics in Austin were better for it. I hitched a ride with a trucker south down I-35, and I've been partying ever since.

"Whoa. You filed an A-127B on me? Son of a —" I peel off the poncho, drape it over my arm, then lean against the window, and ask the question of day. "Since when do we, I mean, *you* watch over fallen angels?"

"You'd be surprised at who all we're watching over lately," Josh says.

That could mean anything. It's good to see him, though. Even after what I did. What was done to me.

Josh's long white gown looks a little less heaven-sent, a little more toga party. His hair hangs in dreadlocks. He's painted his fingernails in alternating silver and gold to match his sandals. He hides perfect wings as an Amtrak employee passes by.

I used to be able to do that—show my wings one minute, make them disappear the next. I used to be able to fly.

I'm dying to know what's up. But Josh can never keep his mouth shut for long. I decide to wait him out.

I do know, though, that his being here means his latest assignment died recently. I don't ask about that. The topic is off-limits. GAs aren't supposed to compare notes on our human charges. We're not supposed to tag-team Fate. I'm tempted to ask anyway, but I don't want to get him in trouble. I never planned to be heaven's bad boy.

But I can tell his loss wasn't that tragic, relatively speaking. Josh still has that peppy attitude of new GAs whose charges have all died of natural causes and in a state of grace. In the early days, before our first assignments, we were so alike.

"You haven't fallen," Josh finally says. "But you have, uh, slipped."

I struggle to register that. "Slipped?"

He takes a breath. "Your powers have been yanked. No flying. No radiance. And you can't carry a tune, not that that's anything new."

Not all angels can sing like, uh, angels. "I know that, so —"

"But," he goes on, "you're still one of us. You can't die. Your veins are full of light, you know, metaphorically speaking. This" — he gestures as if to the whole enchilada of Creation — "is what the archangels are calling 'a time-out.'"

The train car chugs to a stop. Our arrival in Little Rock is announced over the loudspeaker. The hallway fills with underwashed and bleary-eyed travelers.

My stomach turns again. I shouldn't have messed with tequila. Is Josh saying what I think he's saying? "I've been—"

"It doesn't matter where you've been," he tells me, hands pressed piously together beneath his chin. "It's all about where you're going."

"Oh, please. Enough with the cryptic crap."

A big man with a big leather bag, a big belly, a big belt buckle, and big boots looks at us a little too long. Then a girl in a Razorbacks T-shirt says something to her friend about my butt and Josh's shoulders. They dissolve into giggles.

I follow Josh back into my cramped private cabin. I take a seat on the bench. Sniff at the T. Pull it over my head. "Don't get me wrong. I appreciate whatever you're trying to do, but—"

"What is *that*?" Josh asks, pointing at my chest.

I look. "It's a tattoo," I say, just as surprised. "Of a cherub."

A new one. About an inch around, over my heart. It itches.

I resurrect a dim memory of a tattoo parlor. I remember someone making reassuring noises about clean needles and wisecracking about the Roman avatar of love.

"That is not one of the *cherubim*!" Josh exclaims. "That is a fat, naked white baby with wings! How could you do that? Body. Temple. Didn't you read The Written?"

"I've done worse," I say.

We both know it's true. Miranda's name hangs unspoken between us.

Somewhere on the train, a child begins to cry.

"Why are you here, Josh?"

"Michael sent me with a request. He called it 'an assassination of sorts.' If you succeed: do the deed, keep the faith, and, oh yeah, remain virtuous." He smirks. "More virtuous than you've been lately. You may get your powers back. You might get new assignments. You might even get a chance to prove yourself worthy of hauling ass back upstairs."

May, might, might. If I know anything from being a GA, it's that redemption never comes easily or without a price. "Michael wants me to kill—"

"Wipe out."

"Someone?" Last time I checked, angels weren't in the assassination business.

"Some*thing*," Josh clarifies. "Something"—he makes air quotes with his fingers—"of tremendous significance."

The earth is plagued by demons. Lucky me. This one's special. Destroy it and my prayers will be answered. Screw up and I'll be punted permanently. And the Word is clear on that: fallen angels roam the world until Judgment Day. Then they're sent to hell.

I put my head in my hands and rub my temples. I'm a guardian angel, the lowest ranked. Not an avenging angel.

Not an archangel. (Not that it's always easy to tell the difference.) Besides, I no longer have powers. How am I supposed to fight? And *what*?

"What do you say?" Josh asks.

He's asking. Not ordering. My free will is still in play.

"Is that all you're going to tell me?" I ask, glancing up. I shouldn't be surprised that he's gone.

"Yeah, yeah, okay!" I answer in the empty tin box. "Nice seeing you."

Still, I can't help breaking into a smile for the first time since I lost my girl. After all that's happened, it's kind of nice to know that Josh is still Josh.

I open the bag. Rummage through. A few changes of clothes (office and casual), a toothbrush and paste, floss, mint mouthwash, stick deodorant, a razor, a travel-size bottle of shampoo-conditioner, a black plastic comb, a ten-dollar bill, and two cold bottles of water.

A matchbook from Tia Leticia's Salsa Bar sticks out of the breast pocket of one of the lightly starched blue shirts. Inside it is printed an address in Whitby Estates, Illinois. I've heard of the place. It's a lakefront suburb just north of Chicago.

This isn't my first trip to the Windy City. I used to work there.

I remember overhearing a mob boss talk about Whitby Estates, back in the day. He called it "the scariest damn place on earth."

Zachary

IT'S BEEN ALMOST TWO DECADES since I last spent quality time in Chi-Town. Back then I was the guardian angel to my first assignment.

Daniel "Dan the Man" Bianchi was a twice-indicted politician who supplemented his income with "donations for favors" in brown envelopes slipped under doors. He died from a drug-alcohol cocktail mixed by a high-end call girl in a junior executive suite at the Edison Hotel. It was such a shame. He'd been boisterous as a boy, athletic, and close to his family. He'd gone into politics with the best of intentions, but then. . . . Put mildly, I didn't exactly manage to steer him toward good works, good thoughts, a good end.

With Danny, it wasn't his being agnostic that was the problem. Forget what you might have heard. There are no separate corps of angels for agnostics, atheists, Catholics, Protestants, Jews, Muslims, Mormons, Buddhists, Unitarians, Hindus, Druids, Shintoists, Wiccans, and so on. To put a spin on the old saying, it's okay if you don't believe in angels.

We believe in you.

At the moment, I'm on the South Side, holding onto a metal stability bar on a crowded El train barreling farther south, toward the Cermak-Chinatown station. I should be heading north. I got turned around at the station. Worse, I can't even find Whitby Estates on my map.

I'm also tired, achy, and (Amtrak pulled in twelve hours late) sick of trains.

The sun will set soon. Not that long ago, there were a lot of neighborhoods in Chicago that went dicey after dark. Josh said I can't die. That doesn't mean someone can't rob me or torture me or break my kneecaps or toss me into Lake Michigan wearing cement shoes. Now *that* would be a pleasant way to wait for Judgment Day.

On the other hand, the view outside the sleet-dusted window isn't anything like the Near South I remember. It's condo city out there.

Looking for help, I rule out the sleeping man who

reeks of rum and the young guys kicking a Coke can on the floor and the businesswoman reading a self-help book on self-esteem and the middle-aged executive in the heavy overcoat barking into his cell phone and the elderly lady knitting with a Madame-Defarge intensity.

Somebody in hoop earrings, who might be male or female—it's hard to tell—gives me an inviting smile. I consider saying hi.

Then I notice the Gen-X priest fiddling with his iPod on the plastic bench beneath the IN CASE OF EMERGENCY sign. I'm not sure if the sign is a *sign* or a coincidence. I know enough about the universe to go with it. "Excuse me, Father?"

I tap his shoulder, and he takes out the earbuds. "Yes?"

"I'm lost. I was supposed to get on a northbound train and—"

"Happens all the time," the priest assures me. "Where are you trying to go?"

"Whitby Estates. Didn't it used to be on this line?"

His hand moves to his cross. "The trains don't stop there. Not anymore." Lowering his voice, he adds, "One of our more subtle victories."

I shift the shoulder strap of my bag. What is that supposed to mean?

The priest studies me a moment. Then he brightens,

and I realize that, despite my missing wings and slipped status, he can somehow sense what I am. He's the first adult human to do so. It's a rare ability, even among the pure of heart. Little kids are the most likely to spot us. "Father . . . ?"

"Ramos." The priest blinks twice and runs a hand through his hair. Regaining his composure, Father Ramos reaches into his jacket pocket, slips a hundred-dollar bill into my hand, and grasps it with both of his. "Take a cab. Tell the driver to drop you off a block away. If he balks, offer a fifty-percent tip up front." He pauses. "You're going dressed like that?"

Before leaving the Amtrak car, I showered and changed into jeans and a long-sleeved, hooded Bulls sweatshirt. "I guess."

Father Ramos removes the cross from around his neck. He drapes its long chain around mine. "Take this."

Only one kind of monster is well known for fearing religious symbols. The kind I want to think about least, the kind I hate most.

The priest also hands me a business card. *Holy Cross Catholic Church. Winnetka, Illinois.* "In case you need any assistance," he says. "Or a place to stay or . . . or a nice fruit platter?"

I can't help grinning slightly. A fruit platter doesn't sound bad.

Father Ramos is flustered. He didn't board the El train this evening with the idea that he'd have a chat with a guardian angel.

I consider inviting him along on my mission, but I wouldn't want anything to happen to him. I don't trust myself to keep him safe. But the priest will pray for me. I can tell from his voice. The way he suddenly looks ten years younger than when I first saw him. It's good to know I have at least one friend in this town.

The train stops. Its doors slide open, and the priest is lost among the changeover of passengers. Exiting myself, I don't spot him on the snowy platform.

But there is a girl about Miranda's height, build, and age, with almost-black hair, carrying a flute case. Her gaze lingers on my face as she walks by. I almost say something—which would be nuts, considering—but it's not her. When she stifles a yawn, her breath puffs warm. Alive. But they could be half sisters or first cousins.

Miranda. It's not the first time I've noticed a similar-looking girl. There was that one at the runaway shelter, a closer match. Another at a Sixth Street bar in Austin. My "date" for the night bitched me out for staring.

It's below freezing and sleeting. Taking the stairs from the train station to Cermak, I wish Josh had spotted me a pair of boots. My Nikes are already soaked through. That morning, he left me only ten bucks in the Amtrak sleeper cabin.

But now I have the money from the priest, too. No way does a cab across town cost that much. Even with a massive tip. And I'm hungry again. I ate lunch on the train, a hot dog and fries. But they didn't offer seconds, and that was hours ago. One thing about having a corporeal body: you have to feed it on a pretty regular basis.

I halfheartedly jog the short distance down the sidewalk into Chinatown, passing the neighborhood parking lot and new gold-and-green Nine Dragon Wall.

From what I can see, the place hasn't changed much in the last twenty years or so. Only a handful of the low-lying brick buildings feature an architectural nod to the ethnic flavor of the neighborhood. That mostly comes through in the Asian-style lettering on the signs and the ornate red gate.

I duck into a nearby restaurant. It's the kind of place that has black lacquer furniture; plastic-covered red seats; drinks with names like Scorpion, Fog Cutter, and Zombie; and the Great Wall depicted in a cross-stitched mural.

The grandmother behind the desk rises from sliding a phone book onto a low shelf. "May I help you?" she asks with a slight accent. "Party of one?"

I order four egg rolls to go. "Where's the men's room?"

Looking up from the notepad, the lady smiles, smoothes her gray-streaked hair, and shows me to the top of a steep, narrow staircase.

In the dingy, single-stall men's room, I change into a blue dress shirt and black pants, both wrinkled from the bag, and black wing tips.

I trust Father Ramos. If he thinks it's important to dress to impress, I will. Besides, my best bud gave me the duds for a reason. I tuck the cross under my shirt.

Darkness falls, further lowering the temperature. Outside the restaurant, the arriving cab is a welcome sight. I open the door. Navigate the filthy snow-and-ice-packed curb. Slide myself and my bag onto the cracked vinyl backseat.

"Where to?" The cabbie grins, showing a gold tooth in the rearview mirror.

"Um." I draw the matchbook from my shirt pocket. Read off the address.

"Get out," he replies.

"What?"

"Out, out! Get the hell out of my cab!"

"I—"

"What are you, deaf? Go! Move! Now!"

I've barely cleared the car when he peels out, skidding on ice.

As I catch my balance on the curb, I realize I forgot to mention the fifty-percent tip.

Feeling less optimistic, I try to flag another ride. I'm tempted to go back inside the restaurant and grab a table. But generally speaking, we aren't supposed to put off missions from upstairs for a little hot mustard sauce.

Ten minutes pass. I inhale egg roll after egg roll from the brown paper bag. They're fantastic. Pork, carrots, shredded cabbage, the right amount of grease.

The breeze picks up, blowing sleet into my eyes and cheeks. It's like every cab in the city is occupied or, I think as I wave my arm, driven by a blind man. The cold . . .

Enough about the weather. It's Chicago, the Windy City, in mid-April. Anything's possible. It could be eighty degrees tomorrow. Besides, I'm still an angel. Angels are not whiners. Even grounded, laid-off, practically pointless angels.

Almost half an hour later, egg rolls long gone, I slide into another taxi. Raise my voice over a Spanish music station to tell the driver where I'm going.

"Again?" he asks, squinting.

I repeat myself, this time remembering to offer the extra cash.

The cabbie makes the sign of the cross, opens his door, leaves his key in the ignition, and flees down the street like the puppies of hell are snapping at his heels.

"Uh, Josh?" I call from the backseat. "Joshua!"

Nothing. Oh, well. It's not like he's my genie. "Although a hint or two would be nice!" I release a long breath. Josh will show when he wants to, or to be fair, when Michael gives him clearance.

It's not my place to question. The last time I did that, Miranda was ruined.

I should be grateful to the Big Boss for giving me this one last chance.

I should be, and I am.

Glancing at the steering wheel, I would love to write off the whole abandoned-running-car thing to some machination of Joshua's. It would make my life easier if I could "borrow" the cab.

Leaning forward, I kill the ignition. Get out, locking the keys inside.

No need to panic. I trudge back toward the train station. I'll take the El as far as I can and hoof it from there.

It dawns on me then that I need a weapon. I probably would've thought of it earlier, except that guardians are hardwired to protect, not destroy.

Hmm. I should have asked Father Ramos for help arming myself when I had a chance. I'll give him a call if I can't figure out something along the way.

I'm cautiously optimistic, though. It feels good to have a purpose again. And after all, this whole mission is a journey of faith.

Besides, I'm not exactly fresh off the cloud. I've been an angel since the Truman administration, back when Edward J. Kelly was mayor of Chicago.

I've spent as much time peeping at the world as the next angel. I've seen a lot of scary things. Prison riots, pageant moms, Devil's Night, '70s hair, the World Wrestling Federation, the crash of Japan Airlines Flight 123, that bloodsucker Kurt, who nearly killed Lucy back in Dallas . . .

No. No need to go there, not again. If I begin obsessing over that night—over the sweet, fearful sound of Miranda's voice calling out to her friend—I'll be no good to the Big Boss. The mission is what matters now. It has to be.

A third cab pulls up with the driver's window down. It's an old sedan, but freshly painted under the spray of road salt and slush. The cabbie is a young man, and he's giving me the once-over.

Holding my ground, I rattle off the address again. I mention the tip and add that I'll need to make a quick stop along the way.

"Get in," is the answer. "No extra charge."

I hesitate. "You're sure?"

His warm brown eyes gaze into mine. "It is okay. I am good with God."

I'm not about to argue with that.

Once I'm settled in the backseat and we make the illegal U-turn to head north, I begin: "Uh, about that stop, do you know where I could buy a—"

"Weapon?" he asks. "For where you are going?" The

driver pops open the front seat armrest and hands me a sharp wooden stake. "Here."

I slide it up my sleeve. "Thanks."

If I ever make it back upstairs, I owe this guy's GA a beer.

Miranda

OUR HUMAN HIRES, much like the White House staff and funeral directors, tend to have been born into the tradition. Part of it's a matter of discretion. Part of it's the sensibility of those being considered. They've grown up in the business.

Turnover is steady. Humans tend to be fragile creatures, the longest living of them rarely surpassing their eighties, and, for the most part, their physical decline makes them ugly and useless to us long before that. Still, it's safer than one might imagine, working for the eternal royalty and aristocracy. House servants, especially personal assistants, are most useful. Those exceptionally well placed enjoy a higher standard of living than the average eternal, and if approved for elevation, they enter their new existence with the most desirable of connections. A royal servant may become a royal family member someday. It's all very Cinderella-meets-*The Addams Family*. On the other hand, any failure to please may result in a quite literal termination of service.

"Ready, mistress?" Harrison asks. Any other servant would wait for orders, but he can be cheeky that way.

"Send the first one in."

At sunset, I decided to field applicants in my office and slipped on a turquoise chenille sweater, prefaded jeans, and running shoes. With Father gone, it seemed an opportune time to take a break from the Goth glam.

I scan the long, rectangular room. My office is lit by two candle chandeliers, one over my mammoth 1950s-style industrial desk and one over the plush gray seating area. The room is otherwise furnished with floor-to-ceiling barrister bookshelves on one side and more of the same three rows high on the other.

Above the shorter cases, the rock walls are punctuated with matted and framed theater posters—*Little Shop of Horrors, My Fair Lady, West Side Story.*

I considered and rejected *Romeo and Juliet.*

Notepad? Check. Pen? Check. Résumés? Check. Battle-axe? Check.

The latter was a gift from Father. Apparently, every

eternal worth his or her hemoglobin has a custom axe mounted on an office wall (although Father himself doesn't actually bother with an office). Mine is forged of steel. The twenty-four-carat gold inlay handle features a repeating design of dragon heads with emeralds for scales and rubies for eyes. A five-carat, round-cut diamond, embedded in platinum, decorates the end.

Last night before turning in, I asked Harrison to cull through the candidates.

I glance over the application at the top of the stack. Flavius Fielding: age twenty, originally from Peoria, a recent truck-driving-school dropout.

I frown at the typo—an *e* at the end of *Chicago*. The paper is rumpled. A dark-green sticky splotch clings to the top right-hand corner of the page.

I did mention a preference for candidates between ages seventeen and twenty-five, though. Plus, Flavius is a legacy. His grandfather was the PA to our leading Romanian aristocrat.

"Presenting Flavius Fielding," Harrison says.

Flavius, wearing an off-the-rack suit, scurries in and folds himself into the chair.

"When was the last time you washed your hair?" I want to know.

He twitches and reaches into his jacket pocket for a small tin. "Mind if I snack?" He doesn't wait for my reply. Instead, Flavius opens the lid and lifts out a large brown, furry squirming spider, which he shoves whole into his mouth and chews. With his mouth still full, he extends the box in my direction. "Want one?"

Three gooey, mangled arachnid legs stick out from between his stained teeth.

"Harrison!"

"Mistress?" He must've been waiting right outside the door.

"Next!"

"You're not pleased?" Harrison asks, not trying to hide his amusement. "His manner, it's classic."

Classic Renfield, he means. The human servant to Dracula Prime.

Flavius plucks a roach from the box and, in two crunchy bites, eats it, too.

I grimace, wryly acknowledging the PA's joke at my expense, admiring the bravery and stupidity of it. "Too old school for me."

As for the next several interviewees, they may be neatly summed up as awkward, boring, clueless, morose, tedious, needy, obsessive-compulsive, and generically high maintenance.

I'm baffled. This is the royal household. There is no station more sought after. Either the local pool has evaporated to a puddle or Harrison is seriously off his game.

"Presenting Kyle Anderson," the PA offers.

Then *he* walks in. Clean-cut, more cute than handsome and, granted, not tall, but at five foot seven, he still has six inches on me. He wears creased jeans with a wool sweater almost the same color as mine, and he walks right up to shake my hand. He's from the Hyde Park neighborhood and will graduate from high school this spring. His mother is a CPA, his late father taught law, and he looks every bit as toned as soccer star Geoff Calvo. However, the legacy line has been left blank.

"You do realize that this position is unusual?"

He nods. "Right, because you're all vampires."

As they say, fools rush in. "Eternals."

"Sorry, 'eternals.'" Kyle rubs his chin, a thoughtful gesture.

I can't help finding it endearing. Perhaps I can offer a gentler hand within my inner circle. After all, I've been so understanding of Harrison's eccentricities, and in retrospect, his little joke with Flavius tonight inspired my first sincere smile in some time.

"You didn't know," I acknowledge. "You won't make that mistake again."

Does Kyle find me attractive? I wonder. Eternals are more luminous than humans and not only through the eyes of the enthralled.

"How did you come to learn of us?" I ask, standing. "Not eternals per se." Again, we're considered rare, but not fictional. "Rather this household?" I make my way around the brushed steel desk, thinking that if his answer satisfies, I might whisper in his ear that he's mine. That's sexy, right? Ear whispering?

Right then, a stake drops from his sweater sleeve to his waiting palm, and he arches from the chair to strike.

He's not here for the job, I realize. At preternatural speed, I grab the weapon, break it in two, and toss the pieces into my trash can.

"You're too slow to be a hunter," I say, extending my teeth. "Too sloppy."

Kyle scrambles, overturning his chair. "I've been tracking you."

I grab him by the sweater. "Because?"

"You killed my —" He chokes up.

My grip goes slack. "Who?"

"My father," Kyle spits out. "I saw you leaving my house that night. I've been searching for you all month."

It wasn't me. I haven't hunted on the South Side since the Fourth of July. I have killed, but not this boy's father. It must've been someone else from Whitby Estates.

How dare he enter this home under false pretences! How dare he attempt to punish me for what another eternal has done! I toss the Van Helsing wannabe, and he flies across the room. His shoulder cracks as it hits the bookshelves. Then he falls forward, facedown, nose shattering, unconscious on the wood floor.

"Mistress?" Harrison inquires from the doorway.

"How in hell's name did he get past you with a stake?" I demand.

Harrison's eyes widen. "Forgive me, Your Highness! I haven't been myself lately. Please don't tell the master, I beg of you! I swear on my life that it won't happen again!"

"I should hope not!" I say, making an effort to calm myself.

I'm reluctant to punish Harrison. First, he belongs to Father, and the truth is, I enjoy the PA's company. I'm more shocked than angry anyway. Harrison has been nothing but the picture of competence since we met. Granted, his moods have seemed strange lately. His judgment has been a bit off. Yet given the stress of service to the royal family, it's a wonder any of our servants can maintain their mental health.

I won't tell Father about this incident, I decide. Perhaps, though, I'll suggest annual psychological and medical checkups for the staff. In addition, I'll speak to the doctors and ensure that Harrison has a CAT scan, just in case.

"Your Highness . . ."

"Oh, never mind. Let's just move on." I gesture at Kyle. "This one isn't a complete waste. Let's break for an hour. Is Nora's pumpkin bread ready?" At Harrison's nod, I add, "Excellent. Do fetch a bowl and the loaf. I'll take my meal in here."

I'll tear off small pieces of the bread and dip them into the blood of the unconscious boy on the floor, much in the fashion of Vlad.

After Kyle is removed, a maid arrives to clean the excess blood. She pauses outside the open office door, her eyes downcast, and I order her in.

I go to my desk and log onto the Internet on my laptop. I'm doing it to appear occupied, unconcerned about the submissive maid.

She kneels, nearly frantic as she scrubs.

I key in my password, NESBIT, at the ENN site and skim coverage of Father's visit to New York. The photo shows him in Times Square. He's quoted as describing me as his "jewel" and his "sharpest weapon."

After posturing and the political support of the aristocracy, the third most important key to maintaining control of the Mantle is media management. That said, the latter isn't a major challenge. Father has complete control over our press.

Within one hour of breaking the rumor about his alleged mental instability, the entire staff of the *Herald-Gazette* was promptly executed and replaced.

Eternals have no right to speak, to assemble, to anything that I learned about in Government, though everybody seems enthusiastic about bearing arms.

It's a larger, more in-depth feature story than those I've read previously. The article notes that in life Father had three daughters, which is news to me—he never discusses his human existence. A restored and colorized photo of the girls is featured next to my promotional mug shot. They were slender with blond hair and hazel eyes, shown in what I assume are Civil War–era dresses. Perhaps it's merely that their features echo his, but they look familiar somehow.

On one hand, I'm surprised that Father hasn't called to check on me. On the other, now that I think about it, I won't be surprised if he doesn't call all month. Thirty days, give or take, is nothing to someone his age, and it's not as though my human dad called when he traveled.

It occurs to me to wonder if Mom had any trouble getting in contact with Dad on his Alaskan cruise after I went missing, or if she waited until his return and threw it in his face that I was gone. I wonder if he ever sent a second postcard, and if so, whether it was in his girlfriend's handwriting or if he scribbled his last words to me himself.

A grunt diverts my attention from the screen. The maid stands, head down, the handle of her bucket in one hand, a blood-soaked rag in the other.

"You may go." I bite back the "thank you."

Zachary

WHITBY ESTATES is a ritzy old bedroom community. To the extent I can see past the privacy fences and strategic landscaping, the homes are massive and fall into the seven-to-eight-figure range. Discreet signs warn of attack dogs. There aren't any streetlights, but I can see fine. The moon is almost full. I walk the shoveled street. Stick my hands under my armpits to warm them. Scan the scene like a prey animal.

True to his word, the cabbie refused more than a twenty-percent tip. We didn't exactly bond on the ride over, but I've still got the stake he gave me up my sleeve, and I already miss his company.

At the address I got from Josh, I make my way through the open wrought-iron front gate and past the dense evergreens lining the property border. Stop to gape.

A ghostly fog clings to this magnificent reproduction of an Eastern European—no joke—castle. It's gorgeous, enormous, and ominous as hell.

As if on cue, something howls. This is the point in the horror movie, I realize, when any thinking person tears out, full throttle, in the opposite direction.

Sweep the place of the creep factor, though, and Miranda would've loved it. A real castle. She went through a huge girly princess stage when she was four. She even had a tiny tiara. A decade later, wearing her first formal to the Freshmen Sweetheart Dance, she spent the evening watching Geoff Calvo from across the gym. I remember thinking on both occasions that she could pass for royalty . . . in looks, if not in attitude.

Enough. I have to concentrate. So far, I've been doing what I was told. Acting on faith. Still, I'm supposed to be an assassin. I'm going against something so deadly and fearsome that it has been targeted by all that is Holy.

I wonder . . . when Michael decided that I would be sent on this mission, was there some reason it was me? Does *my* judgment matter?

I have a sinking feeling that the cross and stake aren't going to cut it. Should I do research? Case the neighborhood? Investigate the title on the house?

I never used to second-guess myself like this, not even after Danny failed to respond to EMS. As lousy as I felt about the way he lived and the way he died, I'd still done what was expected of me. Even Michael said his fate wasn't my fault. Unlike Miranda's.

The absolute last thing I need is to screw up again.

I take the matchbook out of my pocket. I make sure I'm at the correct address and notice a new note from Joshua on the back. It reads, *Dude, knock on the door!*

It's not until I'm halfway up the long, winding drive-way that I spot the first pair of red eyes. A beastie crouches in the mist and snow.

I keep my head up and maintain the same pace. Try not to show fear, but avoid eye contact. I count six or seven. In the fog, it's hard to tell. They're wolf-shaped but not shifters. Wolf-shaped but not wolves.

Vampires. Just as I thought. I've been sent to take out a heinous vamp. Just one. Orders from upstairs are both vague and specific. Joshua said "something." Singular. He didn't say what.

I think back to the Dallas cemetery. Consider the leech lurking among the crypts. The one who killed Miranda. If the archangel hadn't stopped me, yanked my radiance, I could've flushed him out of the shadows and used it to burn his ass to dust.

Now what do I have to work with? Human-level

strength, human-level speed—at least I'm in good shape—and my wits.

I reach for the brass dragon-head door knocker.

What I wouldn't give for a flaming sword.

The heavy arched door creaks open, and a dapper-looking guy snaps, "Who're you? Are you here about the job?"

I think about it. "Sure."

"And your name?"

Back to question one. "Zachary."

He looks vaguely pensive. "Where's your résumé?"

"I don't have one with me." It's the truth at least. I want to ask what job he's talking about, who's hiring. Who or what I'm talking to. Instinct urges me to play it cool.

"Your last name?" he presses.

I mull over the possibilities. I could be Zachary . . . Scott? Taylor? Beaver? I toss the question back, trying not to seem too concerned about his answer. "Who're *you*?"

"Valid point," he concedes. "And furthermore, why should I be reduced to babysitting?" Whatever that means, he doesn't say it like he really minds.

Inside the soaring entry, Mr. Personality—who's strong for a skinny guy—shoves me against the stone wall. He kicks my wing tips apart and pats me down for weapons. He slides the stake down my sleeve and tosses it over his shoulder, muttering, "Fool me twice, shame on me." Then he pulls the cross from under my shirt, yanks the chain over my head, and drops it into his suit pocket. He takes the Tia Leticia's Salsa Bar matches, too, and looks through my bag. Finally satisfied, he says, "Follow me. Chop, chop."

I have no idea why he didn't throw me to the vamp beasties outside for trying to sneak in a weapon. But it doesn't seem to have occurred to him. Maybe that's normal around here, though. Maybe everyone walks in armed or at least tries to. Or maybe this guy is even worse at his job than I used to be at mine.

My footsteps echo on the wood floors. It's all these hard surfaces. The white stone walls. Twenty-foot ceilings with massive wood-beam supports. The dragon tapestries don't cut it for sound dampening. It'll be tough sneaking up on anybody around here.

We pass through the entry into a grand hall. It's decorated with a mixture of fine art, framed weapons, other varied antiques, and uncomfortable-looking furniture.

The stuffed heads of a wereboar, werebear, werebison, werewolf, and werecat protrude from the walls. I try not to imagine the humanlike faces that once hid behind them. I bet I know where the leather of the seat cushions came from.

A pale girl in a maid's uniform uses a feather duster to clean the base of a brass candelabrum. When I catch her staring at me, she grabs a box of lavender tapers from the floor and flees the room.

"Don't take it personally," my companion offers. "The maids don't say much."

That's when I spot the portrait over the fireplace mantel. Three saucy-looking females in flapper wear, showing a hint of fang. They're clustered around an apparently middle-aged, very alpha male with a serious brow ridge. The master of the house, no doubt. He must be the reason I've been sent. I'm supposed to destroy him. Somehow.

"Who's he?" I let slip.

My escort tracks my gaze to the painting. "You don't know?"

I shake my head.

"Well, this should be amusing. You'll find out soon enough."

Miranda

DRUMMING MY FINGERNAILS on the desk, I decide that I must widen the scope of my PA search beyond the Chicago area, which is unfortunate because I was hoping to find someone who already knew his way around.

I hear a fluttering. Sitting still, I wait and listen. There it is again. I glimpse a bat outside one of my office windows and run to open it. "Go away! Shoo!"

It's not shooing. It's Elina! It must be. She's the only eternal in the area powerful enough to make that particular transformation. She's watching me, spying on me.

The nerve! I knew she would be a problem. It was in her smug manner and the fact that Father called on her to temporarily take center stage at my debut.

Old Blood or no, I can't back down from this kind of insult. Can I?

No, I'm the dragon's daughter, his heir. I've privately wondered if Father named me, a mere neophyte at the time, to both positions because I would be no threat to him personally. Regardless, I can't let challengers, even such clumsy ones, strike at the Mantle through me. If the master must maintain authority over Old Bloods, then so must I.

"Harrison!" Seconds later, I try again. "Harrison!"

He must be elsewhere in the castle.

A maid peeks in.

What do I want? "A broom! Fetch me a broom!"

She runs to obey.

"Elina!" I shout at the faux winged rodent. "How dare you!"

Apparently, my reputation needs bolstering. Old Blood or no, I should have *her* forked tongue ripped out.

A moment later, the maid grunts from behind me, offering a plain kitchen broom.

"Get Harrison!" I tell her, swinging the bristles, and off she runs again.

I catch the side of a wing, sending the bat into a momentary spiral.

"Harrison!" Where is he? He's always been there when I needed him before.

I hear my office door open again—finally.

"Elina, beat it!" I shout. I swing the broom once more, strike her small body, and she soars into the evergreens, toward the lake. "Get out of here!"

Zachary

IT HAS TO BE ANOTHER Miranda look-alike. Only this one has slightly longer hair. She wields a broom pointed up through an open window. She's trying to ward off a pissed-off bird? No, a "bat" that, like the "wolves," has red eyes.

"Elina, beat it!" the girl yells as I cross the room.

The voice is familiar.

She's not. She can't be.

She swings the broom again. Harder. Hits her target with the bristles. Drives the thing away. Shuts the window with a bang.

Miranda, what was once *my* Miranda, faces me. She sees me for the first time. The guy who was always there for her. The guy she didn't know existed. The guy whose fault it is that she's become what she's become. And I see her.

To say death becomes her would be an understatement. It's the confidence, I suppose. My girl shrank from conflict. She didn't go after it with a broom.

In her anger, the beast is glorious. Her nearly black hair has taken on an almost blue sheen. Her sun-kissed skin has gone alabaster. She's the one of us who looks like an angel. And she'll remain this way until the End Days.

I want to rip out my heart and hand it to her. I want to fall at her feet. To hell with the mission. To hell with me. I want to change sides.

Then I smell the pumpkin bread and the blood. I see the plate of crumbs and the bowl on her desk. Notice the stain on her lips. Remember all that *hell* implies.

Miranda

ONCE I'VE DISPATCHED ELINA, I turn to discover that I have yet another visitor.

This one is a heavenly-looking young man. He's tall and muscled like a swimmer or a statue by Michelangelo. No, not a statue—nothing so mundane, so common, as a mere masterpiece. More like its inspiration. His shoulder-length, gently curled hair falls like feathers. It's a golden brown, a shade lighter than his skin. His eyes are a shocking green—not emerald, warmer than that, more vibrant, and fringed with dark gold lashes. He looks like he's been ripped from Eden, and he's gazing at me as if mesmerized, as if he loves me, and as if I'm the most geeky hell spawn in history.

I can almost hear Father chiding me. My visitor is only human, after all—at least irrelevant, possibly dinner, at most a potential pet. Still, it's mortifying, the way he first saw me, swatting at Elina like that. I look so sloppy in the jeans and sweater.

Why didn't Harrison announce him? What is he doing here? Wait. He's seventeen to twenty-five, more like twenty-five. Twenty-two? He's dressed for success, and he's interviewing for the job! That's it! He wants to—it's almost too scrumptious to contemplate—serve me.

I try to dampen my optimism. What if he's a hunter or a bug eater or underqualified? Oh, he doesn't look anything but qualified. Back in my breathing days, I would've been panting.

"Have a seat," I say, gesturing to the chair across from my desk.

He cocks his head as if uncertain. Then, taking his time, clearly wary, he makes himself comfortable.

It's all I can do to stop staring. I swear I've dreamt of him before.

"I don't have your résumé," I begin. I draw the drapes and move from the window. "And you weren't announced." It's my imperial tone, like the one Father uses. It's also an indisputable assertion bordering on accusation. I've been practicing.

The applicant doesn't reply. Instead, he rests his elbows on the chair arms and steeples his fingers beneath his square jaw. It's odd. He's acting like he's being punished.

No matter. Father says it's important to maintain a relaxed dominance. You have the power, but you shouldn't have to work at it. "Your name."

The young man still seems confused, even stunned. "What about it?"

"What *is* it?" I demand, taking deliberate steps. Just when I'm feeling in command, I trip over an untied shoelace and flail toward the desk area.

The applicant springs from his chair, taking a giant step onto my desk, another across it, and lands like a cat to catch me.

I glance at his hands on my shoulders. "Are you a shifter?"

"I'm Zachary," he says. "And no, I'm not a shifter."

I can feel the heat from his skin through my sweater. I place my fingertips over his pounding heart, enchanted by its rhythm, and push him gently back a step. "Zachary," I repeat, liking the way it sounds. "You're here for the job?"

His gaze is steady, but I can hear him swallow. "You could say that."

Why is he being so strange? Is it awe at being in my presence? Nerves over the interview? Or is this some innovative strategy to capture my imagination? "Have a seat." Didn't I already say that?

We take the traditional employer-applicant positions across my desk. "Were you referred, or did you see the job announcement?"

"I was . . . referred."

It's like pulling fangs. "By?"

"Joshua," he answers in a suddenly more confident tone. Like the name itself is reassuring to him. "Joshua Michaels."

I don't recall a Joshua, but I met about a hundred eternals the night of my debut party and it's also quite possible that he's a respectable aristocrat who simply didn't make the guest-list cut. "Obviously, as my personal assistant, you would be expected to do my bidding." It's a great expression, "do my bidding." "Everything from answering the phone to acting as my liaison to protecting my safety to . . ."

"To?" Zachary prompts, raising an eyebrow.

I wish I'd skipped my blood-soaked snack. I feel my blush deepen. "Attending to my personal needs."

By which I don't mean doing my hair.

His smile could launch a toothpaste company. "I'll take it."

I'm flabbergasted. "I . . . It's not up to you to take it. It's up to me to offer it." I did not just say that! "I mean, me." Worse! "I mean, myself." Mayday!

How did he do that? One minute I'm doing just fine. The next, I'm utterly flustered. Oh, who am I kidding? One look at him would be enough to fluster anybody—with or without a pulse. I'll regroup and start fresh tomorrow night.

I draw myself ramrod straight. "You're in luck, Zachary." That wasn't bad. "As it happens, with the master abroad, I have many pressing responsibilities. I'm willing to take you on." Why does every word out of my mouth have to sound so suggestive? "On, um, a trial basis. Yes, you're hired. For now, though, you're excused. Harrison will show you around."

Zachary stands, like he was ready to leave anyway, like he's been toying with me, like it's all he can do to tolerate my presence. "Whatever you say, Miranda."

Zachary

HARRISON MEETS ME in the hall. "Welcome to staff Dracul. Your official title is 'personal assistant to the mistress,' often called 'princess' or 'Her Royal Highness.' Informally, 'Miranda,' but don't presume. She'll tell you how she wants to be addressed."

Nice. He was listening at the door. He already heard me presume. Before I can think to reply, he's launched back into his speech.

"Though you will report first to her, understand that I am the personal assistant to the exalted master and, therefore, your superior. I'll show you to your quarters."

Hang on. Did he say "Dracul"? As in Dracula?

Oh, come on! That's the demon in the portrait?

It explains the castle, though. Talk about believing your own press.

Go figure. Dracula himself must've been the one lurking in the Dallas cemetery. Granted, I never got a look at him. Not flat on the ground with Michael's sword at the back of my neck. But why else would Miranda be here? Be called "princess"?

Miranda. I've seen bloodsuckers before, spat on them. I've never loved one.

It's no surprise, what Miranda has become. I suspected from the moment the archangel said "her very soul is forfeit." I knew when I saw Kurt, fangs bared, in the cemetery with Lucy. If Miranda hadn't been killed in the explosion, this would be the fate I'd sealed for her.

For over a year, I've mourned Miranda, dreamed of Miranda, tried to pretend other girls were Miranda, called them by her name, and seen her when she wasn't there. She should be in heaven right now, playing Scrabble and snacking on chocolate-chip cookies with her grandfather. Instead, she's here. And so am I.

Harrison doesn't seem to notice my zombielike state. "The castle is twenty-five thousand square feet. Each floor is composed of four wings, forming a rectangle, with two connecting hallways in the middle—both running north-south.

"The west wing houses the overflow social and

recreational halls; the north, the dining room, throne room and/or ballroom; the south houses the kitchen and the supply rooms; and of course this, the east wing, is our business center. It's locked daily at sunrise and during events.

"The mistress may give you a key to her office. I have an office of my own."

How nice. I wonder if he was this passive-aggressive before the midlife crisis. Harrison's petty attitude, his apparent acceptance of his place, pisses me off.

I like it, the anger. I like it more than the way my knees keep threatening to buckle. Much more than the price Miranda has paid for my screwup. And I like it better than the thought of disappointing the Big Boss again.

"You'll also notice," Harrison goes on, "three interior courtyards opening from the first floor. The largest is in the middle and often used for entertaining. You may peer down on them and across the grounds from the third floor or climb from there up an additional flight of stairs to a rather pleasant lookout tower."

Like I care about the view. "Where is —"

"Situated on the second floor are the quarters of the executive administrative staff: me, the senior PA; you, the very junior PA; Laurie, the chauffeur; Nora, the chef; and the maids, all of whom have recently had their tongues cut out — long story."

As we climb the narrow, curving stairs, I'm suddenly very aware of my own tongue.

"A handyman, Boris, resides in a cottage on the west side of the property, along with our gardener-groundskeeper, Bruno, though the latter is currently overseeing the landscaping at our estate under construction in San Miguel. The dungeon manager generally stays downstairs, thank God."

"Dungeon?" I ask.

"Along with the wine cellar and the majority of our storage space, it's located, as you might imagine, underground. One of the tunnels beneath the building leads from the dungeon control center onto the east grounds so we don't have to parade human stock through the main house."

I grab Harrison's forearm, harder than I meant to. "You're human, right?"

The answering nod is sharp, punctual, and noticeably begrudging.

"You keep people, fellow human beings, locked up here and feed them to monsters?"

He blinks rapidly. "Just their blood." His tone has lost some of its arrogance. "Not the whole . . ." He gestures at himself, realizes what he's doing, and drops his hands. "Not the whole person."

"And you're okay with that?"

Harrison yanks his arm free and resumes talking as if the subject never came up. "Periodically, the area aristocracy will provide their servants on loan to assist us in such matters as preparing a feast, hosting a party, or trimming the trees after a storm. But only a handful of us permanently reside here. Hence the pleasant quiet of floor two."

I'm tempted to say something about his choice of the word "pleasant," but baiting Harrison is a waste of energy. A distraction from my mission. I need to pay attention, assess the situation, and stop letting my emotions get in my way.

Despite the white rock walls and wood floors, the second level looks a lot more modern, mostly because of the electric light fixtures. The whole place has to be wired, though. The first-floor torches and candles are some kind of design statement or a warning. Any vamp that decorates with flame and weapons has to feel indestructible.

"Guest rooms for visiting aristocrats, including ambassadors, are located on the third floor. As is Her Royal Highness's personal retreat. They're currently unoccupied. The twenty-car garage is detached.

"After the spring thaw, you'll be welcome to use the tennis courts with the mistress's permission. Speak to eternals when spoken to. That includes the sentries. Avoid the V-word at all costs." Harrison pauses in front of an arched door that looks like all the rest. He turns the lock with a long, ornate metal key. Hands it to me. "We're in the process of hiring a new security guard. One of the sentries drained the old one."

"Let me guess," I say. "Long story?"

He waves me inside. "Not so long. Let's just say that calling Miranda 'the dragon princess' is appropriate to tradition. However, calling her 'a dragon lady' is considered offensive to the crown."

My quarters make Danny Bianchi's junior executive suite at the Edison Hotel look like a hovel. The living room is furnished with a sofa, oak coffee table with hammered iron hardware, and two oversize brown leather reading chairs with matching ottomans. Double doors open to a dressing room, complete with four copper-bordered oak wardrobes. Another set of double doors opens to the bedroom, which includes an Arts-and-Crafts desk that was once painted green and stripped, a matching spindle chair, two huge arched windows, and a king-size, four-poster bed with green-and-beige gingko-print linens.

My canvas bag is waiting on the corner of the bed. Apparently, Harrison was able to tell by looking that Miranda would choose me as—what did she call it?—her personal assistant and asked a maid to haul up the bag.

"These are servants' quarters?" I ask.

"We prefer 'executive administrative staff,'" he says. "You'll need more clothes, including party clothes. It's up to the mistress to decide if she wants to dress you or for you to dress at all and whether to upgrade your room. The master upgraded mine."

Like I care. "Where is this master of yours?"

"He's the master of us all," Harrison corrects. "His name is Radford, but you will call him 'Master' or 'Majesty.'" He's abroad for the month. He left two days ago."

A month. Looks like I'll have to make the best of this nightmare for a while. I can hardly imagine it, seeing Miranda night after night. But I can't help wondering . . . What is her existence like in this place? Does she ever pine for her lost humanity the way I do for the grace of the Big Boss? Does she even remember who she was?

Miranda

THE FOLLOWING EVENING, my phone rings as I settle behind my office desk.

"Sugar plum," Father's voice purrs. "How are the interviews coming?"

It occurs to me that I don't have many details to share about my new PA. I can't even remember the name of the eternal that referred him. Avoiding the subject seems prudent. "Quite well, thank you. Are you in London already?"

"I'm on our executive jet," Father clarifies. "We're about to take off from JFK, if the international air traffic will let up. New York was a frightful bore without you."

He misses me! I feel a burst of confidence. "I read a feature story about you. It included a photograph of your human daughters. They were attractive girls, all of them." The line goes silent a long moment, and I squeeze my eyelids closed. Regret floods my veins. "I shouldn't have mentioned it. I'm sor—"

"Now, now," Father interrupts. "We're family, and you should know about our lesser, human relations. I drank down the youngest myself during my first bloodlust. The middle girl saw it happen and lost her mind. Then my eldest took her own life. My wife was heavy with another babe at the time, this one a boy. He went on to live to a right old age and father a new generation. My wife, however, died in childbirth."

Not to sound selfish, but I'm grateful that I didn't first rise in Dallas and that I've never harmed anyone who was precious to me.

It's strange. I've never wondered before what Father's immortality cost him on a personal level, at least not beyond the ability to chow down on southern-fried cooking with ease. He's always seemed so formidable, so secure in who he is now. I'm not sure what to say. "We count the nights until your return. If there's anything I can do . . ."

Father responds by asking me to host any incoming visitors to the castle. "Stick to the niceties on the social front. If you're in doubt about a business or political matter, do an informational interview and then report to me. That said, I trust your judgment. Should anyone unduly vex you, respond swiftly and mercilessly. Don't hesitate to use terminal force." This he says in the same tone my mom would use to say: "Be sure to thank Lucy's mother for dinner."

First overseeing the estate and planning the gala and now this! It's another exam—a final exam perhaps, the chance to confirm myself as a worthy heir.

Unfortunately, I already have to admit one complication.

"There was an incident last night," I say. I fill him in on Elina's bat-form spying and my less-than-terminal response. "Given that she's an Old Blood—"

"Not all Old Bloods are created equally," Father assures me. "Elina is too superficial and stupid to pose a real threat. That's why I permit her to stay in town. She has nothing to gain by watching you. I suspect she's merely jealous."

"Of me?" I ask, glancing at the ornate battle-axe on the white rock wall.

The answering laugh is affectionate. "Sugar plum, you underestimate yourself. Don't worry about that harlot. Once I return, I'll deal with her myself. Meanwhile, you take care and keep in touch. I'll look forward to hearing from you regularly."

Zachary

MAYBE IT'S BECAUSE I got lousy sleep on the Amtrak train or because I still can't get into the flow of having an exclusively flesh-and-bone body or because of the shock of seeing Miranda. But it's a half hour past sundown before I'm up and dressed and ready to confront her again.

Last night before going to bed, I hung up the other two blue shirts and black pants from Joshua in the bathroom off my suite. I still look rumpled, but the steam of three massaging showerheads did help smooth out the wrinkles.

When it comes to creature comforts, I've noticed, the perks of this reproduction castle are a lot more modern than the architecture that inspired it.

I'm careful not to cut myself shaving. This whole place is a shark tank. There's no need to stir up chum for the predators. Truth is, I don't know what would happen if a vamp bit me. But I'm in no hurry to find out. I mess with my hair for a couple of minutes. Until it hits me. I'm primping for her. For Miranda.

Ten minutes later, Harrison briefly intercepts me on the first floor, turning into the biz wing. He hands me a manila file. "You're late and you're rumpled. Neither is to Her Highness's benefit or reflects well on this staff. Furthermore, an eternal, Theo, awaits the princess's audience in the parlor. That's his file."

The east hallway is long and wide. Lined with free-standing World's Fair model slot machines and arched wood doors on one side. A large rectangular window looks out onto an open-air courtyard on the other.

I make my way to Miranda's office, skimming the file of paperwork as I go.

"Enter," she replies to my knock.

I doubt it's a coincidence that we're both here. Either I'm supposed to off Drac at least in part because of what he did to her or our spending time together is some kind of test from upstairs.

When I open the heavy door, Miranda rises from the gray sofa. She seems unsure. Insecure. Not that anyone else could see beneath her coiffed surface. I know her, though. I do. Or I least, I did.

Tonight I can't help catching my breath at the sight of her, the pinned-up hair and sophisticated wardrobe. "You look like Audrey Hepburn in *Breakfast at Tiffany's*."

Miranda doesn't acknowledge that. "I trust your quarters are acceptable."

I'm not fooled by the supposedly cavalier attitude. I loved her as a human, but her acting skills never quite took.

"They'll do." I wave the file. "Vamp to see you."

With a curling finger, she beckons to me to approach. Her small chin tilts, and suddenly, I *don't* know her.

Miranda closes the distance between us in a blur, flicking her wrist to poise clawlike nails no more than an inch in front of my eyes.

"Such striking green eyes," she says. "I could scoop them out and put them in glass paperweights, one for you and one for me. You could consider yours a parting gift."

The flash of fear surprises me. I refuse to flinch. "Is there a point to this?"

"Not 'vamp' or 'vampire,'" Miranda clarifies. "'Eternal.'" She pivots and strides back to her desk. She's somehow grabbed the file on her way and is flipping through it. "He can wait," she declares, taking her power seat.

I don't know what she expects after that show. But I'm not going to wimp out. I ignore the lonely armless chair across from her and sit sideways on the corner of the desk instead. It's stupid, but I'm mad at her. Mad at her for dying. Mad at her for being this thing. Mad enough to push my luck and jeopardize my mission. Did Harrison's demeanor piss me off last night? That was nothing compared to how I feel now.

Miranda crosses her legs and turns her wheeled chair at an angle. "Only because you are in training will I tolerate the occasional slip and only for as long as I'm so inclined. I don't have time to baby you."

"Listen," I begin, "I don't know—"

Joshua materializes behind her. Eyes wide. He frantically waves his hands, warning me to can the attitude. Now.

He's right. I know he's right. I grab a notebook from the top of Miranda's desk, steal a pen from the pencil holder, and offer Josh a look of surrender.

He grins and gives me two-thumbs-up before disappearing again.

"*You* listen," Miranda counters. She pauses and then begins again as if nothing happened. "The tone and temperament of castle life is pristine, orderly, sedate, and regal. Father has asked that in his absence—"

"Father?" I repeat. She never called Troy McAllister that. It was "Da," then "Daddy," then "Dad." I was there, too, for every day of it. They'd been great together, before the divorce, anyway. I wonder if Miranda remembered him last Father's Day.

"The exalted master. As I was saying, Father has asked that I maintain the status quo, deal with any visitors . . ." She taps the manila folder in front of her with one finger. Her nails are back to regular length. "Our most pressing short-term concern is planning his deathday gala. We'll work on that together. If there are any minor complications, Harrison will facilitate damage control."

As she leafs through the paperwork in the file, I watch her absently chew her lower lip. She used to do the same thing in her bedroom in Dallas when she was doing her math and at the kitchen table when she was working on a crossword puzzle.

I wonder if she thought about me today, sleeping under the same roof. My dreams of her were less than angelic.

Back in the main hall, the visiting vamp . . . eternal . . . no, *vamp*, Theo, stands on the edge of what Harrison informed me was an eighteenth-century Tibetan rug. Theo is checking out the nearest glass-fronted display of Ethiopian knives. Even with the other collections featured in the room—the Bavarian crystal decanters, Japanese tea sets, mastodon ivory animal carvings, and mounted shifter heads—the knives dominate.

"The mistress will see you now," I announce. It's one of the lines on the cheat sheet of commonly used castle phrases that Harrison gave me last night.

Theo looks middle-aged. Paunchy. Puffy. He could be two hundred years old for all I know or care. He stands, brushing off his pant legs. Runs a forefinger across his front teeth like a toothbrush. "Thank you, dear boy. It's an honor to meet the princess." He waddles after me. "I've committed many crimes." He sounds oddly apologetic, even mournful, especially considering what he is.

"Yeah," I say, leading him to the biz wing hall. "I've screwed up some myself."

Miranda

I PULL UP THEO'S FULL BIO on the computer. He's a newly elevated member of the gentry and recently relocated to Chicago from New Orleans.

An informal stance seems appropriate.

I return to the seating area, fluff the pillows, and flip through this week's human news magazines while I wait. The same global conflicts rage, and the same political parties bicker, which, granted, will have little impact on the undead community.

"Uh, here he is," Zachary says.

It's a far cry from "Presenting Theo." I make a mental note to correct him later.

I tell Zachary to await my call outside the door and Theo to make himself comfortable in the gray-and-black-striped chair beside the couch. The new arrival wears a beige button-up sweater with leather elbow pads over a white button-down shirt and beige corduroys. He was balding when he died and fortunately shaved what was left rather than indulging in the comb-over. In short, he looks every inch the forty-something psych professor that he used to be.

"My thanks, Your Highness," he says. "I'm terribly sorry. I ache at the thought of having complicated your evening. You see, these past few months, I've committed many heinous deeds, wrought havoc on the innocent, become a parasitic plague. When I received the summons, I knew . . . I knew I would be held accountable."

Summons? There was a summons? At least I know why. From the report, I see that Penelope (Harrison's childhood mistress and one of the cochairs of our Neighborhood Watch program) reported Theo for stalking a human girl who lives in the next town. In Illinois, the only approved hunting grounds are within the city limits of Champaign-Urbana, Bloomington-Normal, Peoria, East St. Louis, Rockford, Springfield, and Chicago proper.

I reach for my blood wine.

Meanwhile, Theo drones on about his pain and angst.

"You do know what you did wrong, don't you?" I ask, taking a sip.

"I walk the earth, terrorizing humanity with—"

"Silence," I say. All he has to do is apologize, agree with whatever I say, and go along his scary way. What's so hard about that?

"You're a blessed and elevated being. You have as much right to consume human blood as a shark does angelfish. You are at the top of the food chain. All this regret, this self-flagellation, it's your soul sickness talking." Pushing away the memory of my own misplaced conscience from my time as a neophyte, I spell it out. "The problem isn't that you would've killed the girl or that you wanted to. The problem is that she's not in an approved hunting zone, and besides, she's a JV cheerleader with new-money parents. Her father is a major political fundraiser. He's connected."

Upon reflection, part of me whispers, this isn't the sort of behavior we can continue to let slide.

I set my glass on the coffee table and reach behind the sofa to wrap my hand around the battle-axe handle I positioned for such occasions. "Do you have *any* idea how much twenty-four-hour television news stations salivate over film of missing young blondes?"

"I would miss her," Theo replies. "Miss the very idea of her." Fat tears roll down his ruddy cheeks. "Each of them is precious, unique, like a snowflake."

That does it. "This is not an Anne Rice novel!" I exclaim, bringing the weapon up, pulling it back like a baseball bat, and, in one smooth motion, beheading him with the sharp blade.

Unfortunately, Theo wasn't old enough to crumble into dust. Blood spurts like a fountain, all over my gray upholstered furniture and silver throw rug. I leap out of the way and land unsteadily, in my black pumps.

I didn't know to expect it. I've never seen a beheading before. I guess that's because, like a staking, Father considers them unimaginative. "Zachar—!"

He runs in before I utter the last syllable. "Are you . . ." He takes in the display. "All right?"

I adjust my dress. "It's a messy night. That happens around here." Do I sound suitably nonchalant? Not really. I clear my throat and try again. "I need you to clear out Theo's remains and take them to the crematorium in the dungeon."

Zachary turns slightly green and covers his mouth and nose with one hand to block the enticing smell. "What did he do?"

I lick my lips. "Do?"

He looks down, realizes he's standing on spilt blood, and steps back. "Theo."

"Oh, well, he tried to kill a human girl, which . . ." I'm not inclined to elaborate, and I certainly don't owe my PA any explanations. "Let's just say it's complicated."

Zachary

I FEEL THE SLIGHTEST BIT BETTER about Miranda after she tells me that she beheaded Theo because he tried to kill a human being. Better still after I get the body and head into plastic trash bags and onto a rolling metal cart from the supply room, throw up in one of the half baths on the first floor, and scrub my hands twenty times.

I feel a hell of lot worse when I get off the service elevator in the basement.

So this is the dragon's dungeon. CREMATORIUM has been marked with signs and arrows. I quickly find myself walking through a no-frills prison. Chillingly modern. Antiseptic. Most cells are empty.

I count about forty people, teenagers mostly. A third or so in their early twenties.

From their mutterings, I can tell that maybe half are immigrants or "imports."

Each has been allocated a numbered pen—I'm guessing seven by fourteen feet—with steel bars, white rock walls that match the rest, and gray concrete floors. A sleep platform (no mattress) is mounted to each side wall. Every unit is equipped with a small sink and toilet.

The prisoners are barefoot, dressed in paper-thin light-blue hospital gowns. The kind that tie at the back and hang open. Though the lights are muted, I can make out puncture wounds on their arms, legs, and necks.

Most are sleeping. A few cry softly.

The rolling cart's wheels echo, drawing attention.

As I push the cart by, a boy mutters, "God damn you. God damn you."

He looks no older than sixteen. But he's big. Tall and burly. The kind of guy you look at and think: girth. Future NFL defensive-line material. By human standards, I'm built, but he's huge. We're talking six four, maybe two hundred and fifty pounds.

Three cells down, a girl with vacant eyes, her body folded like a cricket, pounds the bars. Her fisted hand is bruised and swollen, speckled with dried blood. Her hospital gown gapes, exposing a stripe of skin. Twin crusted holes rest a breath above the split of her buttocks. With her spare hand, she reaches to scratch them raw.

Moments later, a pocked man rises from behind a beat-up wooden desk. He's polished off half of a pizza. Deep dish. Sausage, mushrooms, and green peppers.

I've been able to smell it since I turned the last corner.

He introduces himself as Gus, the dungeon manager, and says Harrison has already told him all about me.

"You run this place?" I ask, horrified.

"Hell of an operation, ain't it? We feed 'em once a day. That Nora, she's some cook. Spoils 'em, if you ask me."

I didn't. In the cell block, a toilet flushes.

Gus points to a metal sprinkler mounted to the ceiling. "Water 'em once a day, too, to ward off the stink. We also got temperature control and ventilation and air purification." He motions toward an industrial-looking workstation.

A large console features half-inch toggles numbered to correspond to the cells and what looks like one large master switch. Key cards, likewise numbered, are stored in slots on a panel secured by bolts onto the rock wall.

"Solid cages," Gus goes on, "strong enough to hold most shifters or even a young vampire. These scrawny human brats, they don't got a prayer. You got to keep an eye on them so's they don't off themselves. Last week when I was sleepin', some chick yanked out enough of her own hair to shove it down her throat and choke to death."

I feel like my throat is closing, too.

"In the storage closet, we got ropes for the humans and chains for the spooky types. It's sexier to chain humans, but then they're harder to rip off the walls and —"

"How do you restrain old eternals?" I ask.

He barks a laugh. "You don't."

Joy.

"Furnace is over here," he says, like I wouldn't have noticed it otherwise. He tosses Theo's head into a corrugated cardboard box atop a long metal tray resting on a conveyor belt. "I'll crank 'er up after I finish my pizza."

I help him move the plastic-wrapped body into a larger box.

"If they get sick," Gus adds, "something contagious, we burn the whole stock. The master doesn't like to take chances when it comes to phlegm."

"It's dangerous to him?"

Gus chuckles. "Nah, it just grosses him out."

Excellent. So far I've ruled out mucus as a weapon. "About the puncture marks," I begin again. "The eternals don't kill the prisoners?"

"Depends." Gus wipes his hands on his T-shirt. "We got syringes that work as good as fangs." He grabs another slice of pizza. "Want some?"

I shake my head.

"Suit yourself. The master likes to keep the sentries hungry, mean, and furry. They get theirs in buckets back behind the garage. As for the little princess, her appetite leveled off after the first big wave, and back then she took hers off the streets. She doesn't have the stomach for the kill, if you ask me. Not yet anyway."

He has my complete attention. "How so?"

Gus takes a bite, spends forever chewing, and swallows. "Pretty much it's the master who sucks 'em dry here, and that's only when he doesn't hit the city. But if there's a party, big crowd and all, that can turn into a real bloodbath. Literally." He grins. "Sometimes with bathtubs and everything. We got a few old-fashioned dragon-footed numbers."

I peek at the paperwork on his desk. Numbered columns correspond to occupied cells. It looks like blood extraction is managed. I wonder how long the prisoners are kept.

I clear my throat. "I have a tub like that in my quarters."

"How nice for you, just arrived and already the exec perks. I guess you got the looks for it." Gus seems on the verge of a rant but shakes it off. "So, you know, the tubs are antiques but real nice restorations. We got more in storage."

I almost hate to ask. "Why?"

"A couple of years back, the master had 'em all hauled out to the main courtyard and . . . You okay there? You're lookin' pukey around the gills."

"Go on."

"Let me put it this way," Gus clarifies. "They called it 'a tribute to the Countess Elizabeth Báthory.' You heard of her? Human chick from way back when. She bathed in maidens' blood to keep herself lookin' young and hot. Get it? Bath? Báthory?"

"Hysterical." I can't hide the shudder. "But I don't think that's how the name is pronounced."

A sliver of green pepper is stuck between Gus's front teeth. "Don't sweat it, pal. They don't got another shindig scheduled till the master returns, and anyway, nobody but sweet thing herself is gonna take a bite out of you."

My gaze flicks to his desk again. I spot the order form. He's requesting a delivery of fresh prisoners in mid-May. That's what? Just under a month from now.

I've been telling myself I can hide in plain sight. Bide my time. But it's one thing to order Miranda's paper clips and drop off formerly undead body parts. It's another to play servant boy, knowing what's happening down here.

What the hell is Michael thinking? Where's Josh?

Gus winks at me. "How's life with Her Highness? Some gig you landed, pal."

I can't blow my cover. But I really want to punch him in the face.

That last night in the cemetery, Miranda was barely past girlhood. A dreamer, a reader, an animal lover. Never superficial enough for her mother. Taken for granted by her dad. Ignored by that popular boy, Geoff Calvo. But committed to being Lucy's best friend in the world. A loyalty so strong that it was part of the reason she died.

But what is she now? Does the fact that those theater posters hang in her office mean anything? Does she still care about her human dreams?

What do I really know about demonic infection? Vampirism? Anything?

I walk away. Back down the long hallway toward the service elevator.

"God damn you. God damn you. God damn you," the boy chants as I pass again.

Miranda

STARING AT MY BLOOD-SOAKED OFFICE, I'm reminded that Father admires not only mercilessness, but orderliness as well. Replacing the lounge area—the upholstered furniture, pillows, and rug—won't be difficult. However, Zachary is still off disposing of Theo, and I want everything that's been ruined cleared away immediately.

I hit a button on my desk phone. "Harrison, send in the maids, all of them."

Within three minutes, Charlotte and Lisa (I think) have arrived with buckets and brushes. I direct them to the seating area, and they begin breaking it down without eye contact or hesitation. They're doing their best, desperate to please, but it's a substantial task, especially for only two people. The sofa is heavy. Besides, I didn't request only two of them. I return to my desk and call again. "Harrison?" No response. "Harrison?"

I try another button. "Nora? Have you seen, um, Renée and Katerina?"

"Honey, they . . . They took off before daylight in one of the white vans."

"Off as in . . . ?"

"Skedaddled, hit the road, vamoosed. I think they were waiting for the master to clear town. The sentries figured they were running out for supplies and let them go."

I'm appalled. "Why didn't Harrison tell me?"

Nora is unfazed. "Maybe he figured you were busy with that handsome new boy."

Or perhaps Harrison hoped he could handle it before I found out. This doesn't speak well of his administration of our staff or, now that I think about it, my oversight of the servants as a whole. What will Father think?

It occurs to me then that perhaps Harrison has already contacted Father about the missing maids and that it's equally possible he's also reporting on *my* performance.

They're both unsettling thoughts. After all, Father left me in charge here, and so far, I have a—however gorgeous—mouthy new hire, my office is a bloody mess, and two of the castle servants are on the run.

I beep off and glare at Lisa and Charlotte. They're stacking cushions. I should smite them for their missing sisters or cousins or whatever they are, but then I wouldn't have any maids at all. "Faster! For now, you'll do the work of four!"

"Dinnertime," I announce when Zachary returns from disposing of Theo. "Nora will have a meal ready for you. I remember something about veal tenderloin on the chalkboard outside the kitchen. Typically, servants eat there, but we have so much to do."

Charlotte is rolling up the rug. Lisa just took a load out.

"Obviously, you'll need to reorder furniture and so forth for in here. Do it later. Right now, we have a gala to plan." Glancing at the post-decapitation scene, I decide it's not the most conducive work environment. "Let's move to the formal dining hall. On the way, you can pick up your meal and fetch me another glass of—"

"Some dungeon you've got," Zachary says.

The restrained fury in his voice catches me off-guard. I raise my hand, snapping my fingers once. Charlotte abandons her task and retreats.

"Is there something you'd like to say?" It's the right response, or close to it. Spirit is desirable, but disrespect isn't, and the castle already has Harrison to contend with.

Still, I don't want Zachary unhappy. I'd rather not lose

him. With all I have to do, I need a PA right now. I don't have time to waste hiring a replacement. What's more, I'd never find anyone so deliciously intriguing. Even in the short time that we've known each other, I've been unable to simply default to royal mode in dealing with him. He demands more, and on some level, I've been enjoying that.

Besides, if the job doesn't suit, Zachary can't simply leave. The relationship between an eternal and his or her PA is a lifetime commitment, a till-death-do-us-part arrangement, although the most successful relationships persist beyond.

He sets my striped chair upright. "It doesn't bother you, the people down there? The way you use them?"

I remind myself that Zachary is new here. It took me time to adjust, after all. With training, I'm certain he'll make a capable PA, perhaps even a loving consort.

Father has spoken to me of enthralling humans in the hunt and in seduction. It's not a power all eternals have, and some who do have it consider it cheating. It works best on the weak-willed, the frightened, or those under undue stress. Perhaps Zachary's on-the-job experience tonight has placed him in the last category.

I warm my tone. "I'm sure this is all overwhelming at first."

Zachary hoists the battle-axe, weighing it in his hands. He looks out of place in my office, so clean and pure and hunky against the bloody background.

"What you must understand," I continue, drawing nearer, "is that those humans in the dungeon are there for a reason. It's their natural role."

"How do you know?" he asks.

"I know," I reply. "I know many things." That sounded stupid. "Think of what I could show you, what we could do together." That was worse. How do women do this? Be saucy, be sexy?

"Have you visited them? Talked to them?" Zachary counters. "They're just kids."

I shift my hips, take a few steps in my heels, and wobble on the right one. "Let's speak of the future," I suggest. "Our future. There are castle rooms we've yet to visit."

Rooms with beds, rooms with werebear rugs, rooms not drenched in Theo's blood. Doesn't Zachary find me tempting? Doesn't he *want* me?

"Right now," he says, "I want to talk about the dungeon."

This is going nowhere. He doesn't even seem to realize what I'm offering. But why not? He sought out this job. He sought me out specifically.

Perhaps the wavering eye contact is the problem. I could take his chin and force his gaze to mine. I consider and dismiss the idea.

It's a shame. Here I am, in the company of the most drinkable boy . . .

Oh, well. However intriguing, if he doesn't come

around soon, I can always toss him downstairs with the cattle he cares about so much.

I snatch away the battle-axe, giving up for the night, and reposition it on the sidewall next to the *Little Shop of Horrors* poster. "I'm not merely an eternal citizen or even an aristocrat. I'm royalty. It's unrealistic to expect me or Father, as busy as we are, or the sentries who guard our grounds to go hunting in the city every night. Besides, no one else wants those humans. They're only good for their blood."

"How do you know?" my PA asks again

"I *know*. Nobody ends up here by accident."

He blinks like I've slapped him across the face. Then, as if I'm his own kind, as though he needs no invitation and has every right, Zachary bridges the distance between us and threads his fingers through my hair. When he speaks again, his voice isn't angry. It's comforting. "Are you talking about them or about yourself?"

"They're runaways," I say, batting his hand away. "Or throwaways or shipped in from places more miserable than this. Some are bought outright from their pimps or their parents. What difference does it make? You'll draw from them, too, sooner or later. Or at least that's your goal, right? That's why you're here, isn't it? To become one of us?"

The look on his face . . . It's as if I've wounded him. As if he doesn't know who he is.

Zachary

AFTER OUR SPAT LAST NIGHT over the prisoners, Miranda excused me to enjoy her blood wine in private and summoned the maids back into her office. I suspect that tonight we'll get started on party planning. Put mildly, I'm not looking forward to it.

After what Gus said about the literal bloodbaths, I'm sure we're not talking face painting, fireworks, or pin-the-tail-on-the-weredonkey.

But Miranda isn't up yet. So I take advantage of the lull in my schedule to roll a cart stocked high with cardboard boxes into the dungeon. The boy who last time said "God damn you" as I walked by settles for glaring at me.

"What's that?" Gus asks from his intake desk. He looks up from a handheld video game. It's one of those urban shoot-'em-ups so popular with budding sociopaths.

"Long underwear," I say. "Orders from upstairs. The hospital gowns are tired."

"Little princess doesn't like her food bare-assed, huh?" Gus frowns down at the screen as he's virtually killed. "Eh. The master will just change them to something else when he gets home." He reboots the game. "Have fun."

"Fun" is too strong a word. It makes me feel only marginally better to distribute the new long-sleeved shirts and elastic-waist pants, courtesy of Miranda's platinum card and same-day delivery. I wanted to buy mattresses, too. But I'm already pushing my luck.

About half of the kids ignore me or shrink back when I approach. I drop theirs in the cells. Others waste no time pulling on the duds.

I only wish I could give them some hope to go with the polyester.

"Thank . . . Thank you," mumbles a girl with a Jamaican accent. She slips the pants on under the hospital gown. Turns to the corner of her cell to wiggle into the top.

I avert my eyes, catching a whiff of cigar smoke. I can't tell where it came from.

The next prisoner reaches through the bars. "Gimme, man."

"What's this?" asks the burly guy, the one with the unibrow. "You playin' us?"

"I'm trying to help," I say.

He looks skeptical. But he, too, takes what I offer.

Who are the angels assigned to these kids? Not that they could've necessarily prevented this. At the risk of stating the obvious: crappy things happen to good people. The influence of angels is touch-and-go, and most don't interpret the rules on indirect intervention as liberally as I used to. As I toss out another set of long underwear, I consider the possibility that maybe it was the prisoners' GAs who lobbied Michael to send me here. That, in addition to taking out Drac, I may be the only one who can make all this better somehow. It's an overwhelming thought.

Before I can dwell on it, a guttural noise echoes through the chamber. I look in the direction of the sound. It's Harrison. Drac's flunky. His hair sticks out in every direction. His eyes are blazing red. He's wearing house slippers and a black silk kimono with a crimson dragon embroidered on the back. He's one of them now. A vampire.

Harrison lunges at the first cell and shakes the bars. Roars at the sobbing, half-naked girl inside. He tries another across the hall. Back. Forth. Beyond reason.

It's a tragedy. A life and soul lost. Underneath the snooty exterior, he was a smart, possibly salvageable guy. I'd been planning to try talking him into another career choice.

Now it'll be a miracle if I can escape his raging appetite. I'll never slip past him. I can't outrun him in the other direction either. I've got no place to hide.

As the other kids dive under their sleeping platforms, the big one slides open his cell door and yanks me fast, inhumanly fast, inside and behind his broad back. The door slams back with a clank into what I notice is a broken lock.

At the noise, Harrison looks ahead. Down the long empty hallway. At Gus.

I hear the dungeon manager grunt. Imagine he's hit a broad hip on the corner of his desk. Hear him stumble.

Harrison locks on him like a weapon. Takes him down like a cheetah.

Their bodies crash against the control center.

"Who are you?" I whisper to my formidable-looking companion.

"Brenek," he answers over Gus's gurgling cries.

Miranda

THE RING OF MY CELL sounds incredibly loud in my closed casket. "Miranda here."

"Honey, I'm sorry to bother you. I know we're not supposed to disturb —"

"What is it, Nora? What's wrong?"

"It's Harrison." She goes on to explain that tonight he's risen as an eternal. Gus has been killed, and she and the other servants are holed up in the kitchen.

"Zachary?" I'm already running to the cellar door. "Is he —"

"Just fine, though it was a near miss. He's right here."

I all but fly up the torch-lit stairs. "What happened?" I ask, still on the phone.

"The boy was in the dungeon when Harrison went after Gus."

Zachary's all right, I remind myself. Nora said he was all right. "Near miss" means okay. I just want to be sure. That's only natural. He's my responsibility. Nora, too. All the servants are. I pour on the supernatural speed though the halls, flinging open the steel swinging door leading to the kitchen, and slide in my slippers across the tile.

I lose my balance and wave my arms, trying to catch myself. Zachary steadies me instead. It's the second time he's stopped me from falling. The first was in my office at the beginning of his job interview.

"Everyone's fine," Zachary says. "Harrison took the tunnel leading outside."

I shrug off my PA, my eyes scanning for contusions or puncture marks, before surveying Nora, who's teary, and the two maids, who are crouched side by side, peeking out the farthest window. "Where's what's-his-name?" I demand. "The handyman?"

Again, it's Zachary who answers. "Nobody's home at the cottage. Boris left a note this afternoon saying he was going to the city for a haircut and a new snowblower. I left a message on his cell."

"Why isn't the door locked?" I ask.

Nora wipes her eyes. "There's no lock on it, not that one would help."

Oh, right. Any eternal can break a simple lock or, for that matter, a bolted one. There's not a heavy enough barricade in here that the servants could move to stop Harrison. All these people have for defense is me. I'm guessing that's not their most comforting thought.

I cross to my regular bar stool, rest one hand on the back of it, and pinch the bridge of my nose, trying to think. Father said nothing about elevating Harrison, and I doubt he'd schedule a first rising during his absence.

That strongly suggests he wasn't the one to do it. For a PA to go behind his master's back, especially the exalted master, and drink from another eternal . . . That's unheard of. I doubt the blood was forced on Harrison. He would've told Father, who would've told me. I raise my head. "Harrison has left the property? Do we know?"

"We hope so," Nora replies, blowing her nose.

"What about the sentries?" I ask.

Nora and Zachary glance at each other. She shakes her head. He shrugs.

Harrison could've left as if he were going about his business for the Mantle, but not as a raging neophyte . . . unless it was one of the sentries who elevated him and let him leave. Then again, drinking from Gus should have calmed him. Maybe Harrison did just stroll out the front gate.

I glance at the few (hopefully) still-loyal servants. Zachary has his arms crossed in front of his chest and is looking at me like the whole ordeal is somehow my fault. Nora has moved to the maids, and she hugs each in turn.

How am I going to tell Father? After me, Harrison is his favorite.

I shake my head, frustrated. Is this my responsibility? According to what Father told me, it takes about a month, usually characterized by mood swings and erratic behavior, for the transformation from human to eternal to fully manifest . . . unless, of course, the chosen is killed first during that time (without beheading, fire, insurmountable exposure to holy water, or the piercing of the heart), in which case, the change happens immediately.

Assuming Harrison wasn't a premature kill, though, he must've been initially blessed sometime in mid-March. Yes, I realize, it *was* about then that he began acting differently. Mouthing off within Father's earshot, sending in Flavius the bug eater to interview, failing to detect the young "vampire hunter's" stake. Who knows what other signs I may have missed?

Regardless, I'm the one in charge here now. Our dungeon manager has been killed, and for whatever reason, Harrison is the fourth castle servant we've lost in less than a week.

"Did you call the enforcers?" I ask Zachary, my voice tight.

"The what?"

"Never mind. I'll do it myself."

It shouldn't be difficult for the Chicago-area enforcers to fetch Harrison. I'll order them to leave him intact for us to deal with. Then I'll see what the sentries have to say.

I flip open the top of my cell, remembering the way Flint evaporated in the holy-water dunking tank. I would rather that not happen to Harrison. Perhaps there's a reasonable explanation. Perhaps he'll come home on his own. We are friends . . . sort of.

Shutting the phone again, I say, "No rush."

Zachary

TONIGHT, WE'RE IN a third-floor bedroom. It's decorated in pink and black. It's, hands down, the most girly room I've seen so far in the castle. When we arrived, Miranda proudly told me it had been her nursery, whatever that's supposed to mean.

The last time I looked, she was seated toward the foot of the immense canopy bed, flipping through the Neiman Marcus catalog for party-favor ideas, her feet tucked to one side, sporting leggings and a Chicago Cubs T-shirt at least two sizes too big. It reminds me of how she used to look, except the T-shirt would've read Dallas Cowboys.

I'm standing in only white boxers (with a fanged smiley-face print) behind a tall wooden screen decorated with a heron design, staring at various suits hanging from a coatrack.

"Try the white tux next!" she calls.

It'll look dorky. "And will I get the rest of my barbershop quartet to go with it?"

"You're not to argue. You're to obey."

"Whatever you say, Your Highness." I slide the slacks from the padded hanger. "The coats are all too tight through the shoulders."

"That's your fault," she says, "for having the body of a comic-book superhero."

I'll have to call the tailor again tomorrow.

I used to wish we could be together like this. I'd come up with witty things to say and pretend she could see and touch me as she went about her days.

Under the circumstances, though, *this* is pure torture.

I have one leg in the pants when I smell smoke. I'm thinking cigar. Harrison? "Miranda, do you—?"

"What? Oh, God! Zachary!"

I drop the pants and look from behind the screen to see her pointing at the drapes. A taper must've fallen to the puddle of material on the hardwood, catching the fringe on fire. It spreads fast, snaking upward. Shooting across the heavy checked satin.

You would think vamps would use more flame-retardant fabric.

I'm reminded of the explosion in the West End. Except the smoke is lavender and starting to smell that way, too.

"Are these enchanted candles?" I ask.

"It's possible," Miranda says, moving to a wardrobe. "We get a lot of magical catalogs. You know how it is when your name gets on a list."

A spark lights on the canopy and the mesh goes up. It falls onto the bedspread.

I wave the smoke from my face. Fire can kill vampires. It can kill anything. "Don't you have a sprinkler system?"

"No," Miranda replies. "Too dangerous. Someone could bless the water. We lost a whole sorority of neo-phytes that way at the University of Kansas in the 1980s." She moves from one piece of furniture to another, opening cabinets and deep drawers. "There's supposed to be an extinguisher in every room, but I can't find one!" Miranda flips open her cell and hits a button. "Nora! Fire in the nursery!"

"We should clear out," I say, reaching for Miranda's hand.

She does a double take at my boxers, though it's a safe bet to assume she's the one that had them delivered to my quarters in the first place. "That candelabrum doesn't belong by the drapes," she mutters. "It's always toward the back of the room."

The wool rug combusts at her feet.

"Miranda!" I say, coughing.

This time she goes with me. We step into the hall and shut the door just as Nora exits the elevator with an extinguisher.

"Shouldn't we call the fire department?" I ask, certain the vamps have a class-A volunteer unit.

"We can't," Miranda says. "Then everyone will know."

Fine. I grab the extinguisher, pull the pin, and charge back in.

As the foam sprays, I realize Miranda would've been the better choice for the job. She doesn't have to breathe. But princesses don't do stuff like this.

The blaze may or may not have been mystical in origin, but it's dying out like any would. The door is untouched. The wood floor can be buffed out. Most of the damage is symbolic. Everything that made the room Miranda's is trashed.

Once the fire is doused, I find her seated alone in the hall against the stone wall. Nora has apparently been excused.

Miranda's face is buried in her hands. "Is it out?"

"Yeah." I crouch down to face her. "Are you okay?"

I'm tempted to smooth her hair. I used to do that sometimes when she slept. But now when I touch her, she pushes me away.

"I'm a failure," she says, blinking at my bare chest. "I'm in charge for *five* measly days, and look at all that's gone wrong. Father will be so disappointed. He expects a perfect princess, a perfect heir."

I take her hands in mine and urge her to her feet. "Who cares what he thinks?"

"He's all I have," Miranda replies.

As soon as she says it, I know I'm in more trouble than ever.

I've been kidding myself that I'm just biding my time undercover until Drac comes home. I've been kidding myself that I can separate the Miranda before from the Miranda now. She may think Drac is the only one who loves her.

But she still has me.

Miranda

I IGNORE MY APPETITE, dust my casket twice, rearrange the clothes in my newly installed wardrobe (by color and type), and count the 2,417 bottles of red wine.

Then I take a lavender-scented bubble bath to distract myself from my appetite. Down here in the cellar, Father and I each have private rooms with antique tubs and separate showers.

Later, I fondle the knob of the door leading to the dungeon. I imagine drinking from the vein. The memory of my tiff with Zachary over the bleeding stock stops me. No, the image of his likely reaction stops me.

Untold numbers of humans find the idea of eternal feeding seductive. It would be the one I hire who is repulsed by the idea. Or is it me he's repulsed by?

Not that he's the reason I'm sequestering myself. I keep waiting for the right words to come. The ones that will explain to Father everything that's gone wrong in such a way that he doesn't have me flayed or crushed by a steamroller or displayed under carved wax (all of which he's done to others who've let him down).

I already miss Harrison, and, to a lesser degree, my nursery. It was the one room in the castle that almost felt like mine.

Tonight I hate the U.S. Midwest regional estate.

Tonight I hate the whole underworld.

Father would say I should go hunting in the city, seek solace in blood.

On the other hand, Zachary . . . I'm almost starting to think like him. It's awful. It reminds me of my soul-sick, neophyte days. No matter how much I crave blood, I can't seem to bring myself to call up for a drink.

I keep wondering, though, when I began to accept being an eternal. Was there one moment? I don't think so. It simply became easier with each passing night.

Lacking other ideas, I check my e-mail on my laptop, am relieved to find my inbox empty, and then do a vanity search for my human name.

I pull up a blog called "Missing Miranda." A click reveals that it's something Lucy has launched. I surf around, seeing what's there. Banners. A Web ring. A slide show. Some of the entries are text. Others are video.

She posts memories of me, too, and lists like "12 Marvelous Things about Miranda," as well as statistics and links to worldwide sites related to missing kids and teens. She asks over and over for her visitors to watch for me.

Lucy put so much effort into this, trying to save me. Too bad it's no use.

Today's entry is dated April 20 and titled "Happy Easter, Miranda." The image is from a snapshot of an Easter Egg hunt. We were four, wearing pink-and-yellow lacy dresses, trying to carry egg-filled baskets bigger than we were.

Easter. I hadn't realized the date.

Thinking back, I can almost smell Grandma Peggy's traditional dinner—honey-baked ham and buttered corn and green-bean casserole and mashed potatoes and gravy with sweet iced tea and pecan pie.

Even my parents' divorce couldn't change that. Year before last, Grandma invited Mom to come with me to dinner after morning services on the condition that both of my parents behave (for my sake), and miraculously they did. It was still awkward in a way, forced, though everybody meant well.

Afterward, I called Lucy. She was the only one I could tell all about it, the only one I could count on to understand the good, the bad, and the bittersweet.

I click the comment link and the circle next to *Anonymous*. Fingertips on the keyboard, I stare at the blinking cursor in the empty text box. I type *Happy Easter.*

Then an instant message pops up from drac1.

I'm quick to erase my comment and log off.

Zachary

WITH DRAC GONE, Miranda on hiatus, and no visiting vamps on the itinerary, it's easy to pretend this isn't a place where people are mutilated and sucked dry.

I'm tired, though. Servants of the undead keep a hellacious schedule. We sleep from sunrise to noon and then do our best to handle the daylight errands of our employers. It's a lifestyle built on fear, ambition, caffeine, and five-star cuisine.

I've been making myself useful in mundane ways. The handyman is apparently AWOL (news I'm not eager to pass on), so I oversaw the complete reboot of Miranda's office.

Now, midafternoon, I'm playing sous-chef in the castle's industrial kitchen.

Okay, sous-chef may be overstating it. I'm chopping spuds for Nora's hamburger gravy—commonly referred to by old-school military as "SOS"—over potatoes and toast. It's for the prisoners. Nora claims she gives them meat to keep their iron up.

They're fed like livestock. We're fed like treasured pets.

"Have you heard from Miranda tonight?" I ask.

She stayed in the wine cellar last night. And she's usually out and about by now. She's clearly freaking out over what Drac will think of her "performance" while he's out of town. She used to do the same thing when she was human. If something went wrong, she'd hide out until it blew over.

But Miranda isn't human anymore, and this time she's not only secluded herself. She's also fasting.

"Don't worry, boy," Nora says from the sink. "You'll lure her back upstairs soon enough. You're the best eye candy this pretentious mausoleum has seen in ages. Miranda's had a rough few nights, but she won't sulk long."

Nora speaks with the confidence of the once number-one-ranked chef in the Southeast. Impressive. But it kind of begs the question of why the master vamp would go to the trouble of hiring someone at her level of culinary expertise.

Granted, when it comes to chowing down, the executive staff is spoiled, and it's obvious from the castle and its furnishings that Drac is an only-the-best kind of fiend. On the other hand, the undead as a whole are definitely known more as drinkers than diners.

"Just out of curiosity," I begin, "does Drac ever sample any of your cooking?"

Nora flips on the water faucet to fill a huge stock pot. "You'd be surprised. It's a challenge for him, being an eternal, to eat solid food. But the master's not the type to accept limits. Over the years, he's worked past his gag reflex, and now he can keep down a light meal. He started small, with red grapes and cherry tomatoes." She crosses her arms and tilts her head thoughtfully. "It was quite the moment when he enjoyed his first bite of rhubarb pie since the Civil War."

I grab another potato. "I still don't see why he'd bother. They're not called bloodsuckers for nothing."

Not for the first time, Nora raises her eyebrows at my choice of words, but again, decides not to comment on it. "Ah, but he wasn't always an eternal. When he was elevated, he didn't forget the joys of his human life. Now and then, the master simply wants a taste, so to speak, of the world he left behind. It could be that he misses it."

Nora doesn't say it like she expects me to feel sorry for the monster. She says it like it's important that I understand. That this information about vampires is somehow key. I turn her words over in my mind and find myself thinking of Miranda.

"So," I begin again, "of all the girls in the world, why do you think he picked Miranda to be his princess?"

"No one knows for sure." Nora shuts off the water. "But as a human, he did have daughters of his own. Maybe he misses them, too."

Nora is good company, a great conversationalist. When we first met, she mentioned to me that famous vamps of Chicago history include John Dillinger, "Big Bill" Thompson, and "Bugs" Moran (who never really went to prison—story for another time).

She also takes good care of the staff.

Officially, the castle doesn't celebrate religious holidays. Unofficially, last night Nora, Laurie the chauffeur, and I dined on bacon-wrapped prawns over Gouda grits with steamed asparagus, followed by milk-chocolate *Bunnicula*-inspired fanged bunnies. We said grace, too. (Lisa and Charlotte don't eat in the kitchen. They just nod thanks and take their plates to their rooms. I'm not sure if that's a new thing or not.)

Today the bear-claw pastries on the kitchen island platter were fried at noon. I take a break from chopping potatoes and grab one. "I hope Miranda's not too freaked out."

"The princess?" exclaims Laurie, walking in. "Freaked-out eternals are—"

"The master, sure," Nora says, loading each of the five pro toasters. "But Miranda's just a baby. A baby viper, but a baby nonetheless."

"Yes, precious." Laurie makes a quick circle through the kitchen. She grabs a pastry and a white linen napkin along the way. "How gracious of her to spend the evening in her coffin. If anyone needs me, I'll be in the garage, um, rotating the tires. Or maybe I'll take the limo in for a wash and detailing in . . . Indianapolis."

Taking a bite, I weigh their reactions. I've never had an assignment before that involved quality time with the undead. I'm still figuring out what's the real deal versus what I've filed away from pop culture from Bela Lugosi to *Buffy the Vampire Slayer* (Thank you, Lucy).

Hang on. "Her coffin?"

"It's in the cellar." Nora again. "Usually, the princess and the master spend their days resting there together. They each have their own coffin, side by side."

"I—I hadn't realized," I stammer. I hadn't given it much thought. When I'd heard Miranda spent her days in the wine cellar, I assumed it had been turned into a bedroom.

Nora lowers her voice. "His Majesty is a tad controlling."

Miranda

AT THE DOORWAY atop the curving cellar stairs, I nearly run into Zachary, who's carrying a silver goblet garnished, luau-style, with a tiny yellow-and-orange paper umbrella.

He rocks back, covering the top of the cup with his hand. "If you want to meet in your office tonight, we're green light. It's all spick-and-span." Offering me the goblet, he adds, "I've been helping Nora out in the kitchen today, and I thought you might be thirsty."

"What's this?" I ask. "It smells like . . ." I swirl the liquid, sniff. "It's not human."

"It's cow blood," he replies, tentative.

I should scold him. Cow blood? How ludicrous!

Yet is this an effort to meet me halfway? If so, I think I'm touched. I'd love it if at least this relationship were more simpatico. How to respond?

Zachary's ringing cell phone solves that. He takes the call, answering with a lot of uh-huhs, pacing in the hallway. He's ditched the black slacks for button-fly 501s. The look is casual for the castle, but with that fit, who cares.

I sip the blood, not minding the taste too much.

Tonight will be different, better. Tonight my new PA and I will put into motion the plans for the gala. When I report to Father, I'll lead with that and then break the news about Harrison. Furthermore, Zachary will have the nursery cleaned, just like he did the office, and Father will never know about either mess. We can hire new maids, too (given our resources, replacements with albino heritage can't be that hard to find).

Zachary snaps the phone closed. "It was a PA with a French accent. She relayed a message from her masters, Sabine and Philippe."

"Sabine and ... Are you certain? Those were the names?"

"Yeah, the PA says she's sorry about the late notice and 'asks for an audience.' As in now. If that's not an inconvenience, so long as you're available, with much simpering and groveling. You get the idea."

Just when I thought we'd reached a pleasant lull. It's a touchy situation, politically perilous. A profoundly high-stakes and unexpected test.

When Father said I was to receive guests, I'm quite sure he didn't mean any of this magnitude. Sabine and Philippe can't be brushed off with a mere informational interview, can they? There are pending issues, after all.

I try to call Father, only to reach his voice mail. Zachary is even more clueless than I am. Harrison might know what to do, but he's still missing.

I can't just leave the guests standing at the door. Sabine is considered among the most formidable of the Old Bloods. By comparison, Elina is a minor leaguer.

And yet this is also an opportunity to prove myself, to finally do something right.

"Tell . . ." We're seriously short on staff. "Laurie to let them in and to bring them into the throne room in fifteen minutes." At least she's in her chauffeur uniform. "You come with me."

"Presenting Sabine and Philippe," Laurie says moments later, and bows to excuse herself. Like many eternals, our guests don't bother with last names.

As they enter, I rise from Father's gold-framed and red-padded throne to stand on a raised black marble platform. The room can accommodate five hundred. At the moment, both sides are walled off with red velvet curtains to create a feeling of intimacy. When the curtains are drawn, it doubles as a ballroom.

I consider the new arrivals. There was no need to pull a file on these two. In the underworld, they're the A-list celebrity couple. Everyone knows about them. Sabine and Philippe have long stood proudly at the zenith of the aristocracy, favorites of the Mantle, though their position of late has grown precarious.

In early March, they confessed to Father that one of their handmaidens "accidentally" drained an Italian nun.

Bad form that, nun killing, and the sort of mistake that could be used to recruit a fresh army for the opposition, should the news have reached the Vatican. To complicate matters, a band of hunters was doing a sweep of the immediate area at the time.

Fortunately, Sabine interceded before the body was discovered. She choked it down in wolf form and paid for that with days of vomiting and fever. It's unclear whether the sole source of her misery was the consumption of so much flesh or whether the victim's holy nature contributed.

Regardless, eating human flesh is traditionally looked upon as a shifter activity. For disposal purposes, most of the eternal citizenry, even some of the new-money gentry, travel in the company of werescavengers (Vultures, Jackals, Hyenas, and the like).

Not the royalty or aristocracy. We don't condescend to associate with vermin. We have disposal facilities (like the crematorium in the dungeon) at our business offices and personal residences. All of which is to say, the circumstances in which Sabine and Philippe found themselves were unusual, meriting attention at the royal level.

Father summoned Sabine for a full report, but then Philippe was badly burned when someone, possibly a New Jersey rabbi (it hasn't been confirmed whether he knew about the nun, but cooperative opposition from agents of the world's major religions is on the rise) set fire to their apartment in the Latin Quarter.

The two missed their appointment—one with the exalted master himself—sending twelve bouquets of white lilies in their stead. Worse, they missed my debut party the following month and neglected to send compensatory tribute.

Albeit insulting to the Mantle, it's a credit to Sabine's dedication to her consort that she didn't abandon him in that condition, especially knowing the likely penalty.

They've since relocated to a suite at The George V near the Arc de Triomphe, and though Philippe's face and hands are still covered with shiny scars, preternatural healing has made it possible for him to travel again. Still, he leans heavily on a silver bat-head cane.

It's sad. Philippe was remarkable-looking before, ugly beautiful. According to Father, he was once painted by

Renoir. Still, the cut of his suit is artful. His long, braided hair shines like spun gold. I've heard he's always worn it pulled back, scars or no scars. That must've been how it escaped the flames.

I expect Zachary to follow Laurie out. (I just want my guests to admire him first.) Instead, he takes position toward my front right on the platform, standing with his arms crossed against his chest and his feet shoulder-width apart.

Why didn't I have him change into something more formal or menacing?

At least I'm wearing my lavender slip dress. The bodice is beaded with seed pearls, and a row of black fringe lines the hem of the skirt. It's a coincidence, but Father imported the dress from Paris. Lavender is his favorite color and scent.

Nora told me his human wife sent him off to war with pressed lavender in a handkerchief. For a generation or so, it was all he had of his original home.

"*Bonsoir*," I begin, wishing I'd taken high school French instead of Spanish. Father speaks both, in addition to English of course, as well as Japanese, Romanian, and Russian. The official language of eternals has been English, though, since the early 1900s. "Welcome to the U.S. Midwest regional estate. I offer greetings on behalf of the exalted master. At the moment, he is abroad."

They must know that already. The European eternal media is covering Father's tour, and beyond that, gossip is the number-one pastime among our kind, the one recreational activity—besides feeding and sex—that never seems to lose its allure.

Father's absence is the likely reason they've chosen now to visit. They'll be expected at his deathday gala, and I suspect they'd prefer their status was resolved before his return. I wonder, though, how they plan to explain their choice to seek me out when they readily could have met him in London or Munich.

"*Bonsoir.*" Sabine curtsies. "We apologize again for our indiscretion."

Philippe bows low. "We meant no disrespect."

I'm uncertain how to reply. On one hand, Father expects total obedience, regardless of circumstances. On the other, Sabine and Philippe had unexpected and extreme cause for their failing, they've traveled far to apologize, and they're not run-of-the-mill aristocracy.

Despite the haute couture, Sabine looks no more than fourteen—innocent, delicate, demure. She has the body of a ballet dancer. Her ash-blond hair rests in a twist on her head. Attached to her belt is a black velvet bag, likely filled with the soil of her homeland. She'll use it to sleep on. (Strictly speaking, that isn't necessary, but some of the Old Bloods indulge in the practice.) It was she who'd elevated Giselle, one of Father's lost brides, and Philippe has been Sabine's consort for more than a century.

She's famous for her advocacy for gender equity within

the eternal population, has raised eyebrows by quoting the feminist writings of a human being, Simone de Beauvoir, and it's rumored they had a personal relationship.

Theirs—Philippe's and Sabine's—is one of the few male-female relationships within the aristocracy in which the woman is the public dominant.

The two threw in early with Father against his predecessor in Istanbul when he was a challenger for the Mantle. It's the only explanation I can fathom for Father's not having already eliminated them for their disobedience (or rather had an enforcer attend to it)—that, and the fact that Sabine is the darling of the international aristocracy. No one has a better-placed finger on its nonexistent pulse. Over the years, she has proven herself a valued advisor.

Surely, such loyalty and courtesy merit a pardon. Plus, so far as I've been able to ascertain from the maids'-tongue incident, the question of human flesh has become something of a gray area. And, given what happened to my nursery, I'm inclined to be sympathetic to fire victims.

"We are family," I declare, hoping that Father will be in agreement. It feels right, though. After all, this wisp of a girl is effectively my step-*grandmère.*

"*Merci*, Your Highness!" Sabine clasps her hands. "We bring tribute now!" She calls to her entourage, waiting outside the door.

A subordinate enters and hands a mahogany window box to Philippe, who presents it to me. I'm not surprised to see an antique knife. Father's collection is renowned, and the last time the two visited, they brought a knife originally owned by the Marquis de Sade. This one, however, somewhat resembles a boomerang.

"For the master," Philippe says, bowing again. "A kukri knife. It once belonged to Jonathan Harker."

Father has hardly begun educating me about the history of the Mantle, but there are even humans who know this story. "It's not . . . ?"

"It is." Sabine nods. "You hold one of the two knives that killed Dracula Prime."

I study the legendary weapon. Despite what the opposition would deem a heroic past, it's reeking of evil. I can feel it, rising in waves.

I set the handcrafted box behind me on the throne. I suspect it's not the proper thing to do (I'm not even sure I should've been sitting on the chair myself), but no one here will dare to correct me.

"That is not all," Sabine adds. "We did not forget our princess." She claps her hands loudly twice. "Something special for you!"

From the hallway, two of their men bring forth a teenage guy. He's fresh, familiar. Very familiar . . .

Zachary coughs.

My "gift" is Geoff Calvo from Dallas, the goalie of my high-school soccer team. The boy I'd pined over since the seventh grade. Talk about compensatory tribute! And fetching Geoff from Texas is a valid reason for them to have come to the States.

Sabine hasn't been a real girl since she chose elevation over the guillotine, but she remembered and researched. She brought me what was once my dream.

It's fun to contemplate. I could bless Geoff, elevate him. Or I could keep him forever in my thrall. I could order him to worship me or to, say, wash my car.

I'm standing behind Zachary on the marble platform, so I can't see his expression. Is he jealous? Is he worried that Geoff might replace him as my PA? Or is he judging me again, on the theory that I'll make Geoff a snack?

Geoff himself looks battered, his face bruised, his Fighting Coyotes T-shirt torn. I wonder if he recognizes me. He didn't know I was alive when I *was* alive. Does he know me dead?

"Miranda," he breathes. "I thought you were . . ."

I have a sudden image then, what it must've been like at my high school after I disappeared. It's not the kind of place where things like that happen. I imagine there were prayer groups. I remember reading about a candlelight vigil on Lucy's blog.

Did Geoff light a candle for me?

"Help," he gasps. "Help, please."

Part of me wants to. The rest is reminded of my audition for Juliet and the way he kissed Denise after she and her friends mocked my performance.

I descend from the platform and walk forward to stand in front of Geoff. He falls readily under my thrall. I could crush his throat between my fingers. I could drink it dry between my teeth. Expectation fills the room. I have to make a decision.

"*Merci,*" I tell Sabine. "Your research is impeccable, but alas, outdated. In the past year, my tastes have changed."

Her hand flies to her mouth. "If we have displeased you—"

"It's all right," I say with a flip wave. My guests' anxiousness makes them malleable, which is fortunate because I'm overdoing it. Aren't I? Or maybe my acting skills are finally starting to improve. "I see no need to mention this to the master. Next time we'll try harder, won't we?"

Sabine and Philippe assure me they will and thank me for my benevolence. I'd feel vaguely guilty for manipulating them if I didn't know that their career goals include killing more people than heart disease.

"Put the boy on the royal jet, bound for DFW Airport. See that he is not further harmed or in any way touched by fang. First, though, I wish a moment alone with him. Now leave us be."

Sabine and Philippe exchange a relieved glance, likely calculating that their offering hasn't been a complete failure after all. They make a few last supplicating noises, curtsy and bow, and depart with their entourage.

"Miranda," Zachary begins.

"Hush. I'm thinking."

I feel compelled to do something about Geoff, what he's seen, what he's suffered.

"You will leave this castle the way you came," I begin. "Cooperate with your escorts, board the plane, and be seated until disembarking in Dallas. At that time, you will retain no memory of the events that transpired since shortly before your capture. Call your parents. They'll retrieve you at the airport."

I'm still thirsty—a goblet of cow blood is only so filling—but fortunately for Geoff, I can wait. As a compromise, I bite my bottom lip, lick my own blood, and rise to my tiptoes to kiss his cheek. "You may go."

As Geoff leaves—his eyes still glazed—inspiration strikes. I add, "Oh, and another thing." He pauses. "In the future, if you ever catch any tall, gangly, B-list, geeky girls staring at you, be nice to them. Nothing fancy. Just say hi." I think of my once best friend, who misses me. "And if one of their names is Lucy Lehman, give her a chance. She might be better for you than that skank you took to Homecoming."

Geoff shuffles out of the throne room.

After he's gone, Zachary takes a seat—it's more of a sexy sprawl—on the platform stairs. "What *is* it with you and that guy?"

"I . . . It was a long time ago." Not that long, but so much has happened.

"Why did you let him go?"

I try flirting. "What do you think, Jiminy Cricket?"

"I think it wasn't a very dragon-princess thing to do."

One downside to my growing affection for Zachary? It infringes on my diet.

Later that night, I make a show of yawning and returning to the wine cellar, wait until I'm certain my PA has turned in, and then pad barefoot in my black silk robe and cat yoga pj's into the kitchen.

"Good evening," I say in my best Hollywood vampire voice.

"Your Highness!" Nora exclaims, dropping the sponge she's using to clean the counter. "If I may say so, honey, you're getting too good at that." She puts a hand to her heart. "What can I do for you?"

Climbing onto a bar stool, I wrinkle my nose. "I'm thirsty."

"Hmm." She slips behind the kitchen island, placing it and the cutlery between us. "I just noticed this afternoon that the blood wine has run out. Normally, I'd call Gus, but—"

I clear my throat. "I'm looking for something a little less human."

Nora taps the counter twice. "Than Gus?"

"Than what he served." I pause. "We don't have to

mention this to Zachary. Or to the master." I don't want to think about what Father would say if he finds out.

He'll be home in three weeks, give or take.

Nora takes a sip from her "Kiss the Cook" coffee mug. "Laurie could make a run to the twenty-four-hour grocery for some pig's blood. You might like it more than—"

"The cow," I reply, pursing my lips. Real eternals drink humans. It's our right. It's been done for centuries. It's . . . I just can't make myself. At least not right now.

Nora reaches for her cell. "You've got it bad, hon."

I blink. "The thirst?"

"The boy," she replies. "Zachary."

"Oh, him," I cross my legs. Better that she thinks of me as a love-struck teenager than an eternal defanged. Better still that we chat about something else. "I'm more concerned about the gala. It's an enormous job. I've heard that weddings, for example, take a year to plan. So many decisions and details, and it's vital to Father that it go perfectly."

"Like your debut." Nora tilts her head. "What all do you think he did for that?"

"Nothing," comes the answer with a dawning understanding. "Father is royalty. He delegates. Of course he does. And so will I. Nora, I could just kiss you!"

The chef's gaze drops to my teeth, and she takes a giant step back. "Really, honey, your thanks is enough."

Zachary

THE DETACHED, HEATED GARAGE at Castle Drac is home to a black Caddy, two stretch limos (one white, one black), a black convertible Porsche, a forest-green BMW, two Harley-Davidson motorcycles, two speedboats, a white van, a small fleet of SUVs, and . . .

"You drive a Beetle?" I ask.

"Your point being?" Miranda shoots back.

"Oh, come on." Our banter is lighter than it's ever been. Despite her legendary crush, she let Geoff Calvo go. She's stayed on the animal blood since, and that was three nights ago. Good signs, all of them. Plus, Miranda gave Laurie the evening off and said she wanted to drive us herself. Call me cautiously optimistic. I think Miranda and

I might actually have fun together. "A vamp behind the wheel of a VW Bug?" I reply. "It's adorable."

Did I mention the pink daisy in the bud vase on the dash?

"It's 'eternal,' not 'vamp,'" Miranda reminds me, but this time she doesn't seem to mind so much. "The Volkswagen is not my car. It belongs to Laurie. It's her personal vehicle." Miranda gestures to the mammoth machine to the far right. Black exterior, red racing stripes. It's the largest of the SUVs. Anywhere. "This is mine."

I laugh. "Because a Hummer just wouldn't cut it?"

Each space is marked with a number. Miranda's car is in space two.

I climb into the shotgun seat as Miranda hauls herself up behind the wheel. She perches on a thick yellow phone book so that she can see over the hood.

No way am I going to mention it.

"What *is* this thing?" I ask.

"It's a 1987 Impaler," she replies, turning on the ignition. "It's a classic."

"It's huge. How much does it cost to fill up?"

Miranda pulls out of the parking spot and turns to exit. She presses a button on her dashboard to raise the garage door. "We're *eternals*," she says again, emphasizing the euphemism. "We are evil. We are not fuel efficient."

I smirk. "Did you make a joke?"

"No."

O'Conner's Bar & Grill is an upscale version of one of those chain restaurants with fake antiques on the wall. It's located in the hundred-story Hancock on Michigan Avenue. From what I remember, it's the third-tallest building in the city. I first visited the place with Danny when it went up in 1970.

Earlier tonight, I suggested O'Conner's because I knew the area (or at least I used to), because it's in Chicago's über shopping corridor, and because its Dallas branch was Miranda's fave. But they don't take reservations, and the lobby is packed.

Once we push through the crowd, Miranda amps up her thrall. "We're next," she says. "Table for three."

"Table for three," is the hostess's monotone reply. She grabs menus.

I shake my head. "Look out, Jedi."

For the first time, my girl smiles at me. Miranda is more into fantasy. But her dad, Troy, is a sci-fi fan. So she's seen all the *Star Wars* movies. She knows her *Doctor Who*. She thinks that *Deep Space Nine* is the best *Star Trek* series and that *Firefly* is sorely underappreciated by the masses.

In middle school, I tried to steer her toward the fandom kids. Lucy was already into the scarier stuff. But it never took. Miranda watched that crowd. She envied how they built their own worlds. But she stayed in Lucy's shadow.

The hostess calls, "This way." In her J.Crew long-sleeved black turtleneck, black jeans, and short, sleek pony-tail, Miranda looks like any fresh-scrubbed, Goth-lite girl.

Then a Gold Coaster wrapped in a full-length sable elbows in front of us. "Now, wait just a minute!" she exclaims. "We were here first."

Miranda's eyes go red.

The matron cringes and clutches her husband's thick arm.

"Sorry," I mutter, passing by. "She's got a big appetite."

When we're seated, Miranda glances at me over her open menu. "Freddy will be here any minute, but if you're starving, go ahead and order."

I'm tempted to ask what makes her think I'm hungry. But around the castle I'm getting a rep for my appetite. Part of it's to stay in Nora's good graces and part of it is that I'm still new to earthly pleasures: food, drink, sleep, sex, the basics. Plus, since coming to Castle Drac, I don't get enough shut-eye and fornication is out of the question. It is.

"Not everybody is on a liquid diet," I reply.

When our waiter arrives, I don't bother to look up from the menu. Instead, I order a light beer, mushroom-and-cheese quesadillas, chicken nachos, blackened shrimp fettuccini Alfredo, and a side of corn succotash because it's fun to say *succotash*. I'm thinking about the chocolate volcano for dessert.

I glance at Miranda. She's gaping, practically drooling. At the waiter.

"Will that be all, dude?" Josh stands there in an O'Conner's uniform with a small notepad and ready pen.

"Dude?" he repeats, and I notice he's tied his dreads back.

"No," I say. He shouldn't be here. Or, to be exact, it's okay if he's here. Invisible. Not walking around taking food orders. Now that I think about it, he shouldn't have shown himself in the Amtrak train hallway either. I'd just been too surprised by his visit and distracted by what he had to say to realize it at the time. "I mean, yeah. I mean, we, uh, have somebody else joining us."

"We'll split the quesadillas," Miranda breathes.

If she eats two bites, I'll be impressed. Still, I think back to what Nora said about how, among other aspects of his human life, Drac misses eating food. I suspect that the same is true of Miranda.

As Josh saunters off, she isn't the only one watching him go.

One of the bigger angel perks is our looks. The toned bodies. The hair. There's something about the hair.

At the next table, a young cutie stands in her too-short hot-pink suit and writes what's probably her phone number on Josh's hand. At the nearest booth, a bearded guy waves a napkin. Josh grabs it with a grin and, still walking, waves back.

Once he's lost in the crowd, Miranda asks, "What's your secret?"

I do a double take. Did Josh somehow blow my cover? "What?"

"Don't you ever gain weight? Not to be rude, I'm simply asking. When I was a human, I never could've eaten like that. Werehippos couldn't eat like that."

I laugh. "There's no such thing as a werehippo."

That's when Freddy, the events guy, shows up. He looks exactly like Harrison, except his hair is bleached and he's wearing wire-framed glasses. By "exactly," I mean *exactly*. They're identical twins.

Miranda stands, and there's much cooing and air-kissing before they settle down.

"Okay, let's talk gala!" Freddy says, playing with his PalmPilot. "May 13, 14?"

"We put the fourteenth on the invites," she says.

"Hmm, we're already at about twenty days," Freddy observes. "Not a problem. We have the venue. With Nora, we don't need a catering staff. If she wants, though, I'll nab her some backup from servants in the neighborhood. I'm thinking a 'love bites' theme—sit down, music—harps maybe."

"Harps?" I cut in.

"Father has a passion for country music," Miranda says. She blinks rapidly and adds, "A closeted passion that I didn't mention, especially as pertaining to the collected

201

works of Johnny Cash." She glances at me. "Johnny wasn't a vampire. He just liked to wear black."

"Dancing?" Freddy goes on, as if our exchange never happened. "We can scatter dime-size rubies on the buffet table or maybe sapphires if you're thinking red is over-done."

"So overdone," Miranda says.

Freddy makes a quick note. "And get this: we serve human hearts, cubed and chilled, with chopsticks over sticky rice on heart-shaped plates." He adjusts his glasses. "Of course, real hearts aren't heart-shaped at all. They're more disgusting and lumpy. Hence the cubing, which solves —"

"You want a drink?" I ask him. I can't stand hearing this and not being able to do anything to stop it. I can't stand that Miranda is a part of this conversation. Besides, I need to talk to Joshua. Now.

"I'd love a —"

"I'll get the waiter," I say.

The diners are a mixed crowd. Execs and young pros. Families. Couples. College students. Tourists. Rounding the centerpiece bar, I dodge five tray-carrying food servers who aren't Joshua. It takes me a minute to realize that the men's room is the most logical meeting place. I find him there.

"Where have you been?" he asks, splashing his face at the sink counter.

"Me?" I check under the stalls. Empty. But the dining room is packed. We won't have this space to ourselves for long. "You're asking *me*—"

"It's hard work, waiting tables," Josh replies. "The kitchen is running slow, everybody wants to substitute something, and hungry people can be mean."

"Since when can you just walk around—"

"Covert-ops exception. No showing off the wings, no lighting up, but . . ." He checks out his reflection and messes with his hair. "I'm stylin.' "

I don't have time for this. "About Miranda—"

"Yeah, after all of your moping, I figured you'd be jazzed to see her again. Cool, huh?" No paper towels. He shakes the water from his fingers. "Uh, except for her now being . . . That sucks. I don't mean sucks like . . . I mean, sorry, dude. I totally—"

"Shut up. Listen. Can a vampire be saved? Can *I* save her?"

Josh sobers and starts reciting from the Creed. "An angel may encourage, may inspire, may nudge, but each human soul ultimately chooses its—"

I sock him in the gut, just hard enough to break his train of thought.

"Ow!"

"We're not talking 'human.' Does *she* still have a soul?"

"Not in the way you mean. There's something hanging on, but it's not the soul of a living human being.

What's left is infected. It's withering, and every time her vamp nature kicks in, it'll wither more until there's—"

Right then two guys in overpriced suits burst through the men's room door. They're bitching that neither of them made partner at their law firm.

The heavyset one knocks his shoulder into mine. His colleague in the questionable tie asks if I've been hurt by "the assault."

Josh is gone. I'm sure he didn't run off to check on my nachos and quesadillas. He's once again taken a siesta from the mortal plane.

On my way back to the table, Freddy passes by, headed to the can. He stops me with a hand on my fore-arm. "My brother," he begins. His voice is different. The way he holds himself. "You know Harrison? You work with him?"

"Yeah," I say. "Well, not anymore. He's . . ."

"So it's true." Freddy's head falls forward. "He's one of them now."

I realize that everything I've seen of Freddy up to this moment has been an act.

"I knew this would happen," he says. "I tried to tell him it wasn't too late to walk away. I guess it's too late now."

Miranda

AT CHESTNUT AND MICHIGAN, we say good-bye to Freddy and I begin toying with Zachary's black wool scarf. It's an excuse to touch him. "I suppose we should be getting back."

"Why?" he asks, bending so his forehead is almost resting against mine. "What are you, a workaholic? What do you do for fun?"

Fun. I have to think to remember what the word means. I've never been one of those girls who lives for shopping, but we are standing on North Michigan Avenue, I'm incredibly rich, and there are still another couple of hours before the stores close. "I do need to get Father a gift for his deathday."

Gift giving isn't to be delegated. Father took pains to explain to me the restoration he had done to the Impaler so it would be ready for my debut party. He's harder to shop for, though. There should be a catalog, *For the Exalted Who Has Everything.*

"Let's hit a bookstore," Zachary says. "Or two."

We half walk, half run across all six lanes. We're flanked by business people—men in business suits, dark trench coats, Florsheim shoes, and women in skirt suits, dark trench coats, gym shoes (their pumps tucked into their briefcases).

As we weave through the crowded streets, a cherubic trio of little kids—two girls and a boy, joined by one of those child leashes—stop on the sidewalk. They giggle and point at Zachary. He grins and waves.

I wonder if he wants kids someday. I wonder if that'll stop him from choosing elevation, if it's offered. There's precedent for eternal parenthood, but it's rare, dangerous, and mystical. I haven't had a period since I died.

"Hi." Zachary squeezes my hand. "I'm right here. Where are you?"

"I'm right here, too," I say, making an effort to appreciate the night, the moment: Zachary's calloused hand and the exhaust of bumper-to-bumper traffic, the lovers in horse-drawn carriages and the skyscrapers jutting like fangs.

I breathe the chill into my limp, neglected lungs, setting my stride to the tune of a street musician's saxophone.

He's accepting donations in his open instrument case, set at an angle on the sidewalk. As we walk by, Zachary reaches into the pocket of his black leather jacket and tosses in a twenty. "I love music," he says.

Before I know it, we're in a bookstore, and the spell survives when he lets go.

For an hour, perhaps more, Zachary and I wander, skimming spines, flipping through pages, reading quotes on dust jackets. I leaf through a book on the care and feeding of gerbils, wondering how Mr. Nesbit is holding up. It's not his basic needs that I'm worried about. I'm certain Mom is feeding him and refilling his water bottle and cleaning his cage, but she won't pet or talk to or play with him. That isn't her way.

It's been a while since I read anything but the news or *The Blood Drinker's Guide.* Last fall, I took a couple of online college classes, but with this spring's social calendar, Father encouraged me to take a semester off. Even so, he's supportive of my continuing education. He himself earned an MBA online.

When Zachary moves to another aisle, I pick up a copy of *Curse of the Cubs.*

My gaze strays to a lone blonde wearing a V-neck long-sleeved T-shirt, her hair pulled back in a clip. She studies a volume in POLITICS as I study the skin above her jugular. It looks smooth. I suspect she uses self-tanning lotion.

With a sigh, I shake off the lesser temptation in favor

of Zachary's company. It's hard to even think about feeding when he's around. The section sign reads THEOLOGY, and my PA has seated himself on a footstool, his nose buried in *Angels to Zombies.*

"Sounds more like occult," I muse.

Zachary looks me in the eye. "Do you believe in angels?"

"Angels?" It's an odd question. I know Clarence from *It's a Wonderful Life,* and the Bible is chock-full of winged guys who start sentences with "lo." Lucy's mom has this old-fashioned framed picture of a floating guardian angel, overseeing two children—a boy and a girl—crossing a bridge. Or maybe they're on train tracks—I don't remember for sure. When I was little, I used to imagine I had my own guardian angel, sort of like an invisible friend. "Seems like wishful thinking."

Zachary slips the book—subtitled *The Apocalypse A to Z*—onto the shelf. He reaches for another one, resting on the floor beside him. "Here. Try this."

Wow the Crowd. It's a book on acting. Grandma Peggy gave me a copy one year for Christmas. A remarkable coincidence, but Zachary probably deduced my love of theater from the framed posters hanging in my office back at the castle.

As we pass the in-store coffee shop, I ask, "Do you want to stop in?"

He replies, "How 'bout we go dancing instead?"

Zachary

I'VE SURPRISED US BOTH. I want to dance with her, though. Just once. The universe owes us that. Besides, she's never had a real date. It's not that guys didn't notice her. Though she held back, my girl had a faerie-like beauty and shy sparkle. But her obsession with Geoff Calvo was as transparent to the masses as it was a pain in the ass to me.

At the checkout counter, we have the books shipped to the castle so we don't have to carry them. Outside, back on the sidewalk, the temperature hovers at around forty degrees. But Miranda doesn't seem to notice, and I'm okay. The wardrobe she had delivered to my room included a black leather jacket worthy of James Dean.

A CTA bus rolls by. A young couple strolls arm in arm, speaking Russian. Two pissed-off-sounding guys, one behind the other, shout threats at each other and kick at pigeons on the sidewalk. A fair-skinned, distinguished-looking man carrying a black umbrella tips his hat at me as he walks by. I consider hightailing it to the 900 Shops on North Michigan to pick out dressier clothes for the occasion. But the castle is so much about wardrobe. I like the idea of looking like regular people.

We hop a cab with no shocks south to the Edison Hotel. As the cabbie complains about the Bulls, Miranda snuggles against my arm and her thigh presses against mine. I doubt she's doing it on purpose.

Miranda apparently still has no experience with guys. I, on the other hand, am decades older. Plus, I let it rip, drowning my sorrows in earthly pleasures in the months before I woke up on the Amtrak train. But she's really getting to me.

I hold it together as the cab passes the Tribune Tower and the Wrigley Building. At Millennium Park, I shift in the seat and clear my throat. Finally, I take her hand and gesture toward the Art Institute. "I'd like to take you there sometime."

Once the words are out, I realize I mean them.

"I'd love that," she says, like we're a normal couple. "How about next week?"

White lights dot trees growing from the medians and

along the sidewalks. Old-fashioned-style streetlights glow golden. It's a romantic night.

But Miranda and I, whatever we're doing, it can't last. According to the Auto Shop and Body Repair calendar stuck to the cab's dash, Drac will return in just under three weeks.

Now that I know where he sleeps, I can't help wondering . . . When I destroy him, will she try to stop me? How big of a dent have I made in her loyalty to the master vamp?

I know the Edison Hotel because it was Danny's fave hangout. I'm relieved to see the sign. Good news. It's still in business.

"What do you think?" I ask as a bellhop holds open the thick glass door.

"Swanky," Miranda says.

The 1927 twenty-five-floor hotel has a forty-foot lobby ceiling, comfortably worn antique furniture, breathtaking crystal chandeliers, and an A-list clientele. Babe Ruth, Charles Lindbergh, Amelia Earhart, and a mixed bag of heads of state, including every president since FDR, have stayed here. The carpet is red, the walls gold, and the columns carved from gray marble. Even the trash cans are made of gray marble.

It's the kind of place where you expect to see a slinky doll with a long white feather in her hair walking a cheetah on a thin gold leash. It's also off the supernatural grid. Or at least it was back in the day. I can't think of a better, safer place that would welcome both of us.

Miranda

IT'S NOT LIKE THERE aren't any grand historic hotels in Dallas, but my family didn't go to places like this. When my relations came to visit, they stayed at our house. When we visited them, we stayed at theirs.

I've been to one wedding reception, my cousin Molly's, and it was at a Doubletree or someplace like that in the San Francisco Bay Area. I also was invited to Shira Levine's bat mitzvah at the Marriott in Plano because our moms are friends. They were nice hotels, clean and new, but not the kind of places where you could imagine running into movie stars or presidents or, now that I think about it, undead royalty.

Zachary accompanies me up a sweeping red carpeted staircase with gold banisters to a four-star, candlelit seafood restaurant with a generous dance floor off the bar area and a five-piece band playing old love songs. We're underdressed — me in my black turtleneck and black jeans, Zachary in a white, long-sleeved shirt and black cargo pants — but no one seems to mind. I free my hair from the ponytail, glad I wore the three-inch dress boots tonight. I'll stick with my higher heels from now on.

When we take our places among the swirling couples, most of them in their sixties or older, he looks at me, sheepish. "Uh, do you know how to dance?"

I can't help smiling. The moment I'm feeling out of place, Zachary reassures me that we're not so different. I relax against his chest, my cheek on his shoulder, and breathe him in. Zachary smells so good, like vanilla and musk. Like sex and Creation. Or at least what I imagine them to be.

Somehow, he knows most of the songs.

"I can't sing worth crap," he says.

I'm playing with his feather-soft curls. "Most people can't."

He sidesteps. "Not most *people*, that's true."

We seem to float between the dance floor and our table.

When Zachary spills red wine on his white shirt, it's an excuse to fuss over him with soda water, to bring my lips close to his, until he draws me up to dance again.

I'm not the only one who admires him. Everywhere we've been tonight—at O'Conner's, at the bookstore, on the street—humans have noticeably marveled at Zachary's beauty. It doesn't bother me, though. After all, he's mine to keep.

Finally, we're the last couple on the floor, and the bartender is putting the chairs upside down on the tables. The band stopped playing a few minutes ago. A hostess turns on the vacuum cleaner.

As we exit the coat-check counter, arm in arm, inspiration strikes. At just past two AM, most of the human world may be sleeping, but it's still early for us. "Let's stay here tonight."

Zachary stumbles. "I don't know—"

"Please. I want to pretend like I'm alive."

Saying the words out loud was hard enough. I won't make it an order.

He runs a hand through his thick hair, blinks at me, and, for a heart-wrenching moment, looks away. "Just tonight," he says.

When I show the hotel manager my Dracul platinum card, he hastens to assign us to the bridal suite, no charge, and says he'll put us down for a late checkout.

Moments later, perched on the gray marble counter in

the bathroom, I twist to face the Hollywood-style mirror, framed in lightbulbs.

I look paler than usual. I skipped the pig's blood before we left. I hadn't been planning to stay out all night.

"In here!" I call to Zachary, who was flipping through channels when I left him in the seating area. "You need to soak that stain."

What I know about laundry could fit in a thimble, but my mom was big on soaking. More important, it's a workable rationale to get him out of that shirt, an occasion I've been longing for since the night of the fire when I was too distraught to fully appreciate the view. His fanged smiley-faced boxers were fetching, though.

When Zachary slides the shirt off his shoulders, I'm so distracted that it takes me a minute to notice the tattoo over his heart. I must've missed it the night of the fire. I reach out with my fingertips, reminded of our earlier conversation at the bookstore.

Zachary moves my hand from his skin and gently squeezes it before letting go.

"Where did that come from?" I ask. "The tattoo, I mean."

He runs water over the wine stain. "Austin."

"You were in Texas? Are you from Texas?"

What with the stress of pleasing Father and warding off batty Elina and beheading Theo and dealing with the runaway servants and Harrison's bloodlust rampage and the nursery fire and the French and negotiating my diet and meeting with Freddy, I've neglected to look deeper into Zachary's background.

"I was in Austin before Chicago. I was in Dallas before that."

Virginia artifacts aside, Father doesn't encourage references to human lives. We've had only that one phone conversation about his human daughters, about that aspect of his past. However, he's not here. He's not even on the continent. "I'm from Dallas originally. Wouldn't it be funny if we were there at the same time?"

Zachary massages soap into the stain. "I don't think this is coming out."

I take the hint and try another line of inquiry. "Why the tattoo?"

His smile is wry. "Would you believe I was so drunk I don't remember?"

"You don't remember getting a baby angel tattooed on your chest?"

Exiting the bathroom, he says the oddest thing: "There's no such thing as baby angels. Angels are created full grown and look the same forever."

Like eternals. No, that's a blasphemous thought. If there are angels, they're not like eternals at all.

I follow Zachary into the suite, where he lounges on the sofa. The lights are all on, the television is turned to a dinosaur program, and he's flipping through the room-service menu.

"Do you want popcorn?" he asks. "It's a twenty-four-hour kitchen."

I'm briefly reminded of movie nights with Lucy. The mood here is different, though. Much. "Buttered," I say. "And a bottle of Shiraz." I'll pretend it's a blood mix.

While Zachary—still shirtless—phones in our order, I channel surf. *Urban Cowboy* wouldn't be my first choice. However, the hotel only offers a handful of channels, the movie is romantic, and I miss seeing people in boots and hats.

I douse the lights.

"It'll take forty-five minutes to harvest and pop the corn, uncork the bottle, pour the wine, and bring it all up on an elevator," Zachary says, amused. Glancing at the screen he adds, "I love this flick."

Zachary

WHEN I TOOK THE SHIRT OFF, I figured there would be a complimentary robe. But the closet is empty. I ask for one when I call room service.

By the time I hang up, Miranda's found a movie to watch. The Texas setting of *Urban Cowboy* fits in with my theory that she's homesick. She misses the girl she used to be.

Sissy and Bud are dancing in their wedding duds at Gilley's when Miranda begins tracing my collarbone with her index finger. This time when she touches my chest, I can't bring myself to stop her. Using the remote, she turns off the movie.

I was there when Miranda took her first breath. Her baptism. Her first step. On her first day of school and when she had the chicken pox. In the middle-school girl's locker room when Denise Durant made fun of her bra size. In algebra when she mooned over Geoff Calvo and got a C. When she wrote *BFF* on Lucy's arm cast and when she adopted Mr. Nesbit. I was there when Grandpa Shen was buried with military honors. When Miranda chickened out of going on the Steel Eel. When her MBA dad and beauty-queen mom told her that their fairy tale had gone bust.

The night, maybe the moment when Miranda was closing out the cash register at the mall movie theater and, suddenly, I realized that she wasn't a little girl anymore and that I didn't just love her. I was *in* love with her, too.

Tonight the bridal suite of the Edison Hotel is lit by the glow of city lights. They shimmer against a Baccarat chandelier and reflect in the mirror over this sofa.

Tonight I kiss Miranda for the first time. I taste mocha and black pepper from the wine. Heat from the mango salsa. The kiss is tentative. Uncertain.

It doesn't feel wrong.

Then she says, "It's one thing to die a virgin. It's another to be an undead one."

It's her turn to initiate a kiss. Miranda sweeps her tongue across my lower lip. Through the turtleneck top, her small breasts press against my bare chest. I inhale.

Expect the lemongrass scent of her onetime body wash. She smells like lavender instead.

I remember Nora lighting lavender tapers in the dining-room candelabra. The master's favorite, the chef explained. Like Miranda. She's his favorite, too. What did she just say? "Die a virgin." "Undead."

I scramble to my feet. It was stupid of me to let things go so far. I may have known her from day one, but Miranda just met me. To her, I may look twenty-two, but I'm a hell of a lot older than that. And together we're impossible. Forget love. Forget passion. The absolute last thing I should do is deflower the undead.

"What's wrong?" she asks. Her fingers go to her lips. "Did I do it wrong?"

"I'm sorry," I say. "I shouldn't have . . ."

She stands. "It's because of what I am, isn't it? Don't you understand? You can join me, if you want to, but I can't go back."

"Miranda, it's not your fault. This wasn't your choice. I know you've done terrible things. Just, have you considered that you could still be —"

"Saved?" she asks like it's ridiculous.

Miranda

I CAN'T BELIEVE we're having this conversation. Why did he interview at the castle? What did he think it was, Gymboree? I hoped Zachary would be mine forever. When he kissed me, I was ready to offer him forever. "Pick someone else to proselytize."

He's not going to work out, and it's not an option for him not to work out. Servants to eternals can't simply quit. They can run and hide and spend their lives haunted by termination orders, or they're sucked dry before they make it off the property. I have to get him out of here. I show him the face of a gargoyle. "Leave!"

"Miranda, please, let's just —"

I shove him, and he flies into the hotel-room door. "Open it."

"You're overreacting. We —"

"If you're not out of here in two seconds, I'll kill you myself."

Perhaps it's shock, but when he doesn't react, I reach behind him, rip the doorknob out of its socket, let it drop from my hand, and toss Zachary into the hall.

"Why did you ever come to me?" I demand. "Why apply for PA in the first place? Why did you kiss me? Why?"

He shakes his head, climbs back to his feet, and turns to walk away.

After Zachary is gone, I sob, hard and ugly, until it feels like something breaks inside. I bend over, take staggering steps, and catch myself against a wall. My fingernails curl into the ornate gold-and-red wallpaper.

I reach with the other hand, higher. Blinking back tears, I'm intrigued. It's as if my body is weightless. I try another hold farther up.

A second later, I'm skittering across the ceiling, down another wall headfirst, navigating my way around the framed print of the Old Water Tower.

It's wickedly unnatural. Like Spider-Man, only much,

much creepier. I'm not a real girl. Until now, tonight was a lie. This is what I am.

"Hello? Hello?" the room-service employee calls, knocking on the knobless door. She pushes it open to enter with a tray of buttered popcorn and a bottle of Shiraz. There's a white robe draped over her arm.

Hanging from a corner of the ceiling, I tilt my head, spiderlike.

She looks to be in her late teens. I admire her hoop-shaped earrings with floating hearts. She's tall, long-legged. I wish I had legs like that.

The girl sets the tray on the desk. Slowly, she looks up at me, like she already sensed a predator.

She's a shifter. A weredeer. Perhaps an Antelope.

It's that deer-in-the-headlights look that tips me off.

The thirst rolls, cascades through my body. Insistent, entitled.

I recall what my minister said back home. They're not people. They're animals in people skin. I wonder what it would feel like to pierce hers. What could it hurt? I'll enthrall her like I did Geoff, and she'll never remember.

I flex, releasing my grip on the ceiling, falling to seize the girl's neck as I land, covering her mouth.

Downy light brown fur ripples across her body. Her ears extend, fold. Her hands and feet collapse into hooves. She tries to buck me off, but I'm stronger and needier.

I don't realize in time that I've drunk too much.

As she dies, the Deer reverts to human form. With my bearing down on her, she hadn't been able to concentrate enough to lock in her shift.

I sink beside her. "I didn't mean to. I thought I could stop."

Popcorn is scattered. Red wine stains the thick beige carpeting. The room smells of both and a hint of meadow.

My cell phone rings, and I grab it, half hoping for Zachary's voice.

"How is my sugar?" Father wants to know. "I haven't heard from you lately."

I glance at the dead Deer. Like me, a vampire took her life. To think, I used to be afraid of people like her. Lucy was right. I was prejudiced.

"I'm fine," I lie. "I tried to call a few days ago, but there was no answer."

"Hmm. And how is your new personal assistant?"

Did I tell him about Zachary? I can hardly remember. Maybe Harrison did, before his elevation. Or maybe Father simply assumes I must've found someone by now.

I can't simply pretend that Zachary never held the position. Too many people have seen him. I could say I killed him, but what if we cross paths again? I feign confusion at the rules. "I gave him a brief tryout, but his references never called back. He's nice to look at, but the world is full of attractive toys."

It's delivered with the attitude Father has been trying to cultivate.

"We don't engage in 'tryouts,'" Father replies. "He's a loose end."

"Not to worry," I say. "I wiped his short-term memory."

I bask in Father's praise of my growing abilities and distract him with news that Harrison is one of us now. "I didn't know you'd chosen to elevate him."

"I didn't," Father confirms.

CHICAGO—Tamara O. Williams, age 21, died at the Edison Hotel in Chicago on April 25 in a work-related accident.

Williams was a graduate of Dorothy Pearl Walker High School in Indianapolis, where she was captain of the girls' varsity swim team. She had been recently accepted to begin studies at the School of the Art Institute of Chicago.

Williams is survived by her parents, Laura and Donald Williams; her sister, Jennifer; her brother, James; her grandparents Alma and Frederick Williams; her grandmother Peggy Richards; her nephew, Ryan; and her fiancé, Marc Wojeck. She was preceded in death by her grandfather Simon Richards.

Funeral services will be held at 1 PM April 30 at the First Baptist Church in Holt, Indiana. In lieu of flowers, a memorial fund has been established in Williams's name at the Art Institute.

Miranda

"HERE YOU GO, HON," Nora says, sliding a fresh champagne glass across the stainless-steel counter toward where I'm seated on a kitchen stool. "It's pig juice and Cabernet."

I take a sip and set aside today's newspaper. I try not to think about how much more satisfying the Deer, Tamara, tasted.

Hotel management covered up my crime. An efficient man with a thin mustache apologized for the mess and switched me to the presidential suite overlooking the lake and Buckingham Fountain. I crawled into the king-size bed in the new room and stayed there until sundown tonight.

When thirst conquered the grief and guilt, when I felt like I might claw through the hotel wall to get at the nearest beating heart, I called Laurie. I asked her to stay put and send a sentry (with a bottle of pig's blood) in one of the limos to pick me up and then drop off one of his cohorts at the Hancock Center garage to drive the Impaler home.

I've been back at the castle for less than an hour.

"You want to talk about it?" Nora asks, resting her elbows on the counter.

I shake my head. She's the only human servant I've seen since I arrived. I'm not even sure I should be here with her. I'm developing a pattern of picking food-service professionals as my fatality victims.

I can't get Tamara out of my mind. I flip to the first page on shifters in *The Blood Drinker's Guide*. It says they're natural, children of God. Tamara was a Deer, but she also was an artist and engaged to be married. She had a grandma Peggy, like I do.

Nora nods at my glass. "More where that came from."

Miranda

THE BLACK-AND-BLUE BUTTERFLY emerges like magic from the dense fog and lights on my palm. "Aren't you early?"

It raises and lowers fringed wings. The answer is no. Spring is overdue.

After a moment, it flies away, and I watch it go from my seat in the lookout tower. I'm not sure what I'm looking for up here—answers, forgiveness, a second chance? I can't see anything tonight.

The castle feels empty. With Father overseas, Gus dead, Harrison undead and AWOL, two maids and the handyman on the run, the security guard recently eaten, and Zachary . . . I have no idea what's become of him.

He's been gone five nights. He hasn't used his cell. There have been no charges on the credit card I gave him. I don't know how much cash he had left in his pocket.

It's strange. I'd grown accustomed to this existence, accepted it more and more with each passing night. No, more than that. I embraced the power. At moments, I even relished it.

Zachary changed that. The longer that I was with him, the harder it was to face the reality of being an eternal. I was starting to act and think like the girl he wanted me to be, like the girl I *was* before Father killed me.

When Zachary left, though, it was like I spiraled into relapse. It was Tamara's bad luck to cross my path just then. I haven't felt bloodlust like that since my first hunt, when I drank that waiter in Greek Town.

"If it isn't a princess in a tower," Nora says by way of greeting. Breathing heavily, she joins me on the hard stone bench and hands me a glass of pig-blood wine. The castle has elevators, but they don't open on the roof. It takes another staircase from the third floor to reach it and then one more, topside, to arrive at this circular outdoor room.

Nora's bundled in the rose-pattered cashmere shawl I gave her for Solstice.

With two of the maids gone, she and Laurie have been helping to deliver food to the dungeon. I haven't said anything to the chef about how she's upgraded the prisoners' menus. No more hamburger gravy. Tonight Father's bleeding stock was served quiche Lorraine.

I take a sip. Nora is keeping me well fed, too. "May I ask you a question?"

She waves her hand through the fog, frowning at it. "You can ask."

I choose my words carefully. I'm not judging. I have no right. "I understand Harrison. He never hid his ambition to become an eternal. He knew what it meant and seemed to crave all it implied. I didn't know Gus well, but . . ."

"He was wacky in the head."

She said it. "Why are *you* here?" I ask. "You and Laurie and the maids?"

"As for the maids, I don't know. They kept to themselves, even before . . ." It's kind of her not to say it. "The other two are gone now, too."

An echoing howl rises up, one of the sentries.

"Good for them," I say, waiting for the rest of the answer.

"They appear to have taken Jonathan Harker's kukri knife," Nora adds.

I suppress a sigh. All it'll buy them is more of Father's vengeance.

We share an uncomfortable silence. Half the contents of my glass are gone before Nora speaks again. "I didn't have a choice, or at least I didn't see a choice at the time.

The master read about my catering business in *Southern Living* and decided to acquire me, like he would one of his knives or antiques or properties."

Like he acquired me.

"I'd been a teen mom. My parents threw me out of the house, and Toby's father, he had other things to do. That didn't stop me none. Over the years, I built up my reputation as a chef. Then the master decided I would come here. He showed me what he was. He knew my Toby was a sophomore at Boston College. He knew Toby's street address. That was over twelve years ago, and the master reminds me now and then that he keeps tabs on my boy."

She doesn't have to fill in the blanks. I notice how deep the lines on her face are. To protect her son, she had to make herself a party to Father's madness. An accessory, a court would say, if the courts had power over us.

"Laurie showed up only a couple of months before you arrived." Nora folds her arms beneath her ample bust. "She's dying. It's a cancer of some kind. It may be too late to treat it." After a pause, Nora adds, "She's somehow related to the master. Her family speaks of him in whispers. He briefly reappears in their lives every other generation or so. Their reputation, their standing, is important to him, and he pours in the money whenever needed. Laurie is afraid to die, you see, and she thought—"

"She thought becoming a vampire would be the answer to her problems."

Nora nods without reacting to my use of the V-word. "What's left of the southern gentleman in him offered her the position of chauffeur while she decides."

"I can't imagine her going through with it, now that she knows what it means." Laurie reminds me a little of myself, or at least of the girl I used to be. "I think she'll cheat him in the end. I think she'll choose . . ."

"A good death," Nora says.

It's an interesting way to put it, but, yes, that's what I meant. I'm grateful for Nora's company. "It's nice of you to spend time with me. More than nice—courageous."

She sets a warm hand on my shoulder. "I've been praying for you."

I'm mystified. Nora knows what I am, what I've done. "Thank you, but why? I mean, considering . . ."

Her smile is thoughtful. "Call it faith."

Zachary

I'M DWARFED BY THE TYRANNOSAUR SKELETON at the Field Museum. Forty-two feet long, thirteen feet tall at the hips. It was found buried in the Hell Creek Formation in 1990.

The last time good and evil went head-to-head, no punches pulled, the dinosaurs died out. Lava flowed in oceans as large as the United States. Tsunamis tore apart the shores. Fire engulfed forests, and the sky turned to ash.

According to *Angels to Zombies* and the scuttlebutt I remember from upstairs, we're shaping up for another showdown. And this lame-ass angel?

I can't even handle one teenage vampire princess. Me, the guy who knows her better than anybody else. After what happened last week between me and Miranda, I feel like I'm the one buried in Hell Creek.

I've spent nights at a South Side homeless shelter (and picked up a shirt and jacket there). I've spent days haunting the city streets.

Someone walks up from behind, whistling. Joshua.

"What do you want?" I ask.

"I'm bored. What is this, intermission? Are you just gonna give up?"

He's wearing a White Sox baseball cap, a Shedd Aquarium T-shirt, and blue jeans. He's cuddling a stuffed woolly mammoth toy.

"She fired me," I say. "It's over."

"*She* fired you?" he exclaims. "Did you forget who you're working for? Or have you changed sides?"

"You know what happened. You know what I mean."

I'm not fooling myself. There were a million things I could've done when Miranda tossed me out. But I'm the one who initiated that first kiss. I don't think I could ever touch her again without risking who I am or at least who I need to be.

Josh motions toward the less-crowded Mammals of Asia exhibit and leads me that way. "Okay, but why are you here at the museum? Most self-respecting angels would've chosen a religious refuge. Like a church, a synagogue, a temple, Wrigley Field."

I'm surprised it took him this long to start nagging.

"What about your mission?" Josh wants to know.

I shush him as we enter the exhibit and pass two young women. One looks too much like Miranda for it to be a coincidence. "You suck at subtlety."

He grins. "Part of my charm."

It's a little darker in here. Spookier. Dead animals are mounted behind glass. They've been posed in pairs, families, small herds. The crouching leopard is alone.

I keep walking when Joshua slides onto a long wooden bench. I keep walking when he plops down on fake suede in the octagonal seating area.

Sounds of wind, crunching ice, and animal calls bleed in from Messages from the Wilderness next door. It might as well be called Messages from the Big Boss.

"Well, let's see," I say as Josh jogs to catch up. "I'm powerless. No wings, no radiance. But big deal! So what if I'm persona non grata at the castle. All I have to do is smite Drac and save Miranda's soul, even though she literally threw me out of her afterlife."

"Is that all?" Josh prompts, smug.

"I know, I know. I've also got to free the prisoners despite the locked cells, the wolfed-out vamp sentries, the twelve-foot wrought-iron fence, and a neighborhood chock-full of bloodsuckers."

"Excellent!" Josh hugs me. "Dude, that's so ambitious!"

"But is it possible?" At his double take, I clarify.

"About Miranda. Her soul. With faith, repentance, and sacrifice, anybody can be redeemed, right? Anybody. She's still somebody. Maybe it's harder for a vamp to be good. But you could say the same of the poor or the oppressed or politicians. She didn't fall, Josh. What she is had nothing to do with her free will. She was taken."

He trails me into a larger, more open room. Past the mounted cheetah family and the small kudu herd. We stop in front of the Lions of Tsavo. Two male lions. Maneless. One stands, paw poised to take another step. The other is positioned low, like he's slinking forward. They don't look like man-eaters. Just curious. Ready to play. The way Miranda looks sometimes. But they mauled and ate almost 140 railway workers along East Africa's Tsavo River in 1898 (I read the sign). That's not typical lion behavior. But disease killed off the zebras, gazelles, most of their prey. And the local humans used poor burial practices. It's a good reminder. You have to be careful with the dead.

"Uh," Josh begins, "there's something you should know." He tucks the toy mammoth under his arm like he's trying to protect it.

"Just tell me."

"You're not totally without hope," he says. "You've still got your looks, your sex appeal (or what passes for it), your immortality, and—this is key—your influence."

That makes sense. Like immortality, it's less a power

per se, more inherent. Plus I've had practice. "Angel on my shoulder" and all that crap. "Your point?"

"For the last week, Miranda's been handling the vampire thing on her own."

I glance at the lions, afraid to ask what she's done. "So, you're saying her soul . . ."

"Sorry, man. You know as well as I do that the Big Boss is a romantic. Heaven itself is rooting for you. But it's not like she vamped out yesterday. She's done some serious wrongs. And you can't save someone else. It has to be her decision. She has to face her own inner monster and do what's right."

Sure, I know that. But Miranda's always been bigger on hiding from her problems than tackling them head-on. Not that this week I've been doing much better.

"From where I stand," Josh adds, "it looks too close to call. Tonight's party —"

I grab his arm. "Tonight's? What do you mean 'tonight's'? Drac's supposed to be on a jet to . . . I don't know . . . Sydney right now!"

Josh's voice lowers. "We rely on travel itineraries provided by the dark master since when?"

Zachary

I STROLL BY WEARING a new backpack. Laurie looks at me from her small windowed office in the castle's detached garage. She's drinking coffee and reading a paperback mystery. "You're back?" she asks over the microphone from behind bulletproof glass.

I hold up the flamethrowers like they're tribute. "Romantic, huh? Most guys go for girls who like flowers."

She sets the book beside a brochure from the Mayo Clinic. "Yes, most do."

At the museum, I borrowed Josh's cell to call Father Ramos at Holy Cross in Winnetka. The priest picked me up outside and drove me to his church. Then he gave me the weapons, the backpack, and the station wagon. No questions asked.

Father Ramos offered to come along, too. But my mission is on the stealth side. He's not the type that could pass for a bloodsucker or even a wannabe. And I wouldn't want to risk losing him.

I exit the garage and head to the castle wall. The tunnel entrance looks like a cross between a storm cellar and Fort Knox. I use the master key, open the door, and walk down the stairs and through the tunnel. It's a narrow, water-stained concrete hallway lit with motion-sensor lights.

Once inside the dungeon, I set the flamethrowers and backpack on what used to be Gus's desk. It's not a sophisticated system. I throw the master switch. The cells unlock.

Some of the prisoners exchange glances, but no one moves.

"Hey! I'm trying to help you escape!" I run to Brenek's cell. "Come on."

"We're not stupid." He shoves aside the door with the broken lock to face me in the center aisle. "Why do you think we didn't make a break for it after Gus croaked? I saved you from Harrison because you don't smell like one of them. But there are bloodsuckers patrolling the grounds. I can't protect everyone by myself."

Brenek is fast. I'm sure he's some kind of shifter. But a toe-to-toe battle between only one vamp and (assuming we're talking predators), oh, a Wolf is even money. Here, we're looking at multiple fiends. What makes him think *he* can protect anybody?

Brenek is clearly the alpha of the group, though—the guy I have to win over. "Drac's back in town." I check my watch. "Or at least he should be any minute. You've got two choices. You run and take your chances against the sentries, or you're hauled to the central courtyard to die for sure."

"Party?" Brenek asks.

"Blowout," I reply.

"We will never make it over the fence," says the girl with the Jamaican accent.

"The front gate is open," I reply. "I just drove through it. It'll be open all night for the guests to come and go." I'm hoping the neighborhood undead will be too preoccupied with party prep to give chase. But . . . "There's something else: this whole town is vamp-controlled." Harrison mentioned once in passing that the no-local-hunting rule doesn't apply to escapees. It's bad news. Enough to quiet everyone for a moment.

"I'd rather die fighting than run," puts in a preppy kid—maybe eighteen. His nose has been shattered. His whole face is a green-and-yellow bruise.

"I'll show you how to use a flamethrower," I reply.

"Easy, Kyle," interrupts a girl to my right, and I notice she looks kind of like Lucy. Only thinner, more hollowed, and sad.

"You've got weapons?" Brenek asks.

I should've mentioned that first. "Two flamethrowers, stakes for everybody." It doesn't sound like much. But guns wouldn't slow down the sentries for long. Bombs would make too much noise. "I brought what I could carry."

A small crowd gathers, debating. The more athletic-looking and more pissed off want to know how many vamps are in the castle. Where they sleep. They want payback.

A girl speaking a language I don't recognize is becoming hysterical.

"She won't leave her brother," Brenek says. "The traders that brought him here broke his leg when he tried to run off. He can't walk."

"So they die," declares another prisoner, following her preppy wingman to check out the weapons. "Some of us will, no matter what."

Brenek moans, and the mixed smell of wet fur and pine and mud fills the air. He falls with a resounding thud, catching his weight on his hands. A rapidly forming beard expands. So does the unibrow. They cover his face. Thick brown hair shoots across his body. He moans again and shakes his head. The muscles bulk out, splitting the long underwear into scraps. His face unfolds forward. His hands burst into clawed paws.

With a silent roar, the werebear opens his jaws.

"Ladies and gentleman," I breathe, "your odds just got a lot better."

The girl who was in the cell next to Brenek reaches to stroke the damp fur. He nuzzles her hand. It's clear why he didn't try to escape. A Bear might have a fighting chance against the sentries, but not with someone to protect. Or, I realize as the rest crowd in—hugging one another—a lot of someones.

Humans and shifters don't always, make that usually, get along. This group is beyond that. They've bonded. Brenek chose not to leave anyone behind.

Badass fur ball with a conscience. I like it.

We make an adjustment in the flamethrower team— Kyle volunteered, but he has a messed-up shoulder. And I relay what Father Ramos told me about working the things.

I'm still trying to figure out what to do with the boy who can't run. If I could somehow sneak him and his sister to the cottage, maybe I could hide them there until Drac's out of the way. Maybe.

I walk with Brenek toward the entrance of the tunnel. He'll be leading the charge.

As I turn to wish him luck, I hear Nora's voice.

"Welcome home, Zachary. Her Highness hasn't been the same without you."

Busted. Laurie is standing with her. I don't blame the chauffeur for turning me in. Her life's on the line after all. Both of their lives are.

They're not vampires. Brenek and I could take them, not that I can imagine it going that way. But the problem is bigger than them. They've no doubt alerted the sentries of the escapees. We're screwed.

"You'll never make it to the front gate on foot," Nora says. "Not all of you."

Laurie raises her chin. It's the most empowered I've seen her, and it sucks that the sudden burst of self-esteem has to come from this.

Then she and Nora open fists overflowing with keys, each marked with the number of a corresponding parking spot.

Laurie adds, "But it's only three minutes to the garage."

The keys go fast. The prisoners with flamethrowers look eager to do damage. The boy who can't walk climbs to ride piggy-back on one of the sturdier guys.

Brenek retracts his shift enough to speak. "Some of us want to stay and fight."

"Get the weaker ones to safety," I say. "They're more important."

It's clear that Brenek doesn't like having to choose. But he knows I'm right.

"About that whole 'God-damn-you' thing," he says, taking point.

"Don't sweat it," I reply with a grin.

"We best get a move on, too," Nora says. "Let's go, boy!"

"What?" I ask as the group files out.

"The master will know we had a hand in this," she explains. "Freddy just called to tell me he's back in town. We've done all we can here, and we don't have much time."

"We'll take my Bug," Laurie adds.

I hear a sentry howl, alerting the others of the breakout. Snarls and barking follow. I glance over my shoulder. "You two go! There's something else I have to do."

In the distance, Brenek roars. A yelp tells us he's landed a blow.

"If you're staying, I'm staying," Nora declares. "You may need my help. Laurie, go ahead and take off without us."

"But—"

"But nothing," Nora says. "I'm not sure that enough of those kids know how to drive."

I didn't think of that, and apparently, neither did Laurie. She scoots out at the end of the line.

It's going to be a long night. But at least this part of the mission looks like a success. All the prisoners are on their way. And now I have an ally in Nora.

I don't get a chance to savor the moment.

"Feeling good about yourself, aren't you?" Harrison asks. His hand rests on Nora's shoulder, friendly-like.

With his new speed, I never even saw him coming. The human Harrison would never hurt Nora. With this Harrison, I can't be sure. My gut says he's bluffing. But vamps are unpredictable. Miranda is proof of that. So's Drac.

I eye the extra stake on the desk. It's no use. I'd never strike in time.

"Let's skip the tedious threats," Harrison says, "and get right to the master's forgiving my little—*cough*—indiscretion because I've brought to light this—"

Nora slams her foot into his instep and elbows him in the gut.

Harrison grunts. He's more startled than hurt. He hops a couple of times. "These loafers are hand-tooled Italian leather!"

Meanwhile, Nora runs to my side. The tunnel is our only chance, and I'm reaching for Nora's hand to pull her along when a swirl of dark smoke rises from the floor. It takes the form of a man and shoves us midway between itself and Harrison.

"You!" It's him. Drac. He looks like his portrait over

the fireplace. "You stole my cars!" His gaze sweeps the empty cells. "And my bleeding stock!"

My instinct is to argue with anything he says. But I'm proud of that.

"Nora," he goes on in a calmer but somehow scarier tone, "we're expecting guests. Go upstairs, get to the kitchen, do your job, and maybe I won't have your son's entrails fed to the sewer rats tomorrow."

She hesitates, glancing my way.

"It's okay," I say, even though it's anything but.

"You," Drac addresses Harrison, "chain my daughter's mistake. Give me ten, fifteen minutes, and then escort him to the parlor. It's time the young lovers are reunited, don't you think? He'll make a perfect amuse-bouche."

I'm not big on languages. But I think that means "tiny appetizer."

I'm not only food, I'm insulted.

"Your Majesty," Harrison begins, "perhaps you haven't noticed that I'm a blessed being. I'm like you now. It was I who rooted out this deception—"

"Who are *you* to speak of betrayal?" With that, Drac turns to smoke again.

Harrison's eyes flash red. "The master will kill Nora for this," he tells me. "Kill her truly dead. What were you thinking?"

"Nora made her own decision," I say. "Nora chose well."

Harrison shoots me a look. Angry. Regretful?

Unarmed, I can't outfight him. I can't outrun him either. For now, I'm stuck. That's okay. He's not my target. Given the tension between him and the master vamp, he might even be a potential ally, and right now I can use whatever help I can find. I decide to take it down a notch.

"If you don't mind my asking," I begin, "why did you bail on Drac, anyway?"

Harrison opens the storage closet. "It was risky, but he kept putting off my elevation. And you know, you turn forty, you think about living forever, and you start wondering if you'll be as pretty if your looks are frozen at forty-three."

As he pulls out the chains, I press, "So, who was it?" Despite everything, I'm curious. "Who turned you?"

"Delta," he replies, securing my hands behind my back.

I'm pretty sure he doesn't mean Delta Air Lines.

At my puzzled expression, Harrison adds, "Delta the sentry. You know, the eternals that guard the grounds in wolf form. Alpha, Beta, Gamma—"

"Delta," I say. So Drac doesn't even call them by real names. "Talk about dehumanizing! I mean, even if they are—"

"Inhuman," Harrison agrees, taking my arm. "Yes, Delta made that very point."

Harrison's unbeating heart doesn't seem to be in it as he walks me down the long row of abandoned cells. Rounding a corner, I ask, "And where have you been all this time?"

"Madison," Harrison replies with a wistful smile. "At an underground spa resort owned by rogue eternals. It's top-notch. I signed up for the 'all-me, all-night' package. That's a facial, a Swedish massage, and an herbal blood wrap."

I just had to ask. Boarding the service elevator, I resist the urge to shudder.

Miranda

AT THE IVORY-INLAID VANITY TABLE in my bathroom off the wine cellar, I sink onto a padded Louis XIV chair and apply my lip liner.

I've got the basic eternal beauty kit: makeup, SPF 50, and (still unopened) sunless tanning lotion. The latter is popular among the gentry, but when I arrived preternaturally pale at my debut party, faux tanning was deemed too garish for the aristocracy.

What with the oddity of eternal reflections, I don't realize Father has materialized behind me until the blade of Jonathan Harker's knife pierces my throat.

"I've missed you," I manage. "Welcome home, Father."

Father. The word tastes false and foul.

Troy McAllister is my father. He's into barbecue and sci-fi and the Dallas Cowboys. He and Mom had a lousy marriage and a worse divorce. He shouldn't have let that keep him away so much. Still, he never forgot a birthday and he offered to pay for summer acting classes and college tuition, and he always remembered to ask Lucy whether she'd seen the latest horror movie. Dad has his faults, but he loves me.

I'll never again think of the master vampire as "father."

I'm not his daughter. Not his princess. Not his china doll.

The Dracula presses the blade, drawing a bright line of blood, which streams down my neck. His voice is at my ear. "I've never been so brokenhearted, so down and disappointed."

I knew he'd find out about everything that had gone wrong, sooner or later. I'd been hoping for later. I still don't know what to say.

"I've been here with you this whole time," Radford announces. "The bat at the window, the extra wolf-form sentry, the dust on the coffins and wine bottles, the passing gentleman on the crowded sidewalk . . ."

The mist in the fog! He was watching me, sabotaging me, *spying* on me.

I'd been wrong to assume the bat was Elina! No wonder he said he'd handle the matter himself. I'd wondered how he could dismiss an Old Blood so easily.

I remind myself that, in his own twisted way, Radford really does consider me his child and he's been acting based on that. I've heard of parents reading diaries, listening in on phone calls, even checking Web-browser histories. This is taking it to the next level. I don't know how well he managed to follow me through the city or how well he can hear in his less-corporeal forms. This was more than a mere surveillance effort, though. He set fire to my nursery. "So," I begin, "your entire 'absence' was a test?"

I'd thought so, but I'd underestimated how intrusive, manipulative, and deceptive of one. The cut isn't deep, not yet. My blood is seeping steadily, though. I look like I'm wearing a red turtleneck.

"That's all you have to say?" Radford thunders, removing the blade. "My cars are gone! My cars and my bleeding stock! Every last human in the dungeon and now Laurie, too. My gala is tonight! I already had Freddy send out the word. The guests will arrive soon. Whatever will they think? Your boy, he's the one responsible! And he turned my own chef against me! She helped him! Damn him to hell anyway!"

Oh, God. "Zachary?" I ask. "He's back? Is he alive?"

"Not for long."

I reach for a washcloth and press it against the shallow

cut. "Pity." With my free hand, I refresh my black lipstick and then reach for a two-inch-thick black velvet ribbon. "He's so nice to look at. Still, he'll make a tasty treat."

I doubt that was the response Radford expected, and I'm proud of having delivered the line so well.

I'm also furious. Strip away his machinations, and all *I* did was make one ill-advised hiring decision. Meanwhile, it's not as though Harrison has been the model PA.

Not . . . Not that *his* standards matter. I've had enough of his monstrous sensibilities, enough of the monster in both of us.

"Yes. Well . . ." Just like that, Radford's demeanor flips and he abruptly changes the subject. "Not so long ago you called the human world home. We must be open to new ideas. Progress is a glorious thing!"

It's dizzying, his mood swing, like that night in the kitchen with the maids' tongues. One moment he's out for my head. The next I'm his "sugar" again. Only this time, his madness is working in my favor.

"When hosting a fete," he goes on, "what do young ladies and gentlemen of limited resources offer their peers?"

It takes effort to decipher Radford's question. "You mean, what do people serve?" I think back to the one big high-school party I attended. "If someone has a fake ID or an older brother, they might get a keg. Usually, it's BYOB. Bring your own—"

"Body!" Radford exclaims. "What a jim-dandy idea!"

Now what did I do? "It is?"

"This traitorous behavior by our staff, we can't stand for it! As royalty, the burden falls on us to send a message across the board. The humans' foolishness will cost lives, and"— he snaps his fingers —"satisfy our need to supply a more complete menu. Our guests can drink the pets they bring with them. Sugar, you're a bona-fide genius!"

I can't believe he never left! I can't believe the party is tonight! I have to hurry. Radford said to dress for the gala and meet him in the parlor in five minutes.

Radford said that Nora helped Zachary free the prisoners. I'm not surprised. I think, for her, doing something like that has been a long time coming. I suspect it was delivering the food to the dungeon herself, facing those victims in person, that finally pushed her to act.

I'm also sure she wouldn't have crossed the line without warning her son first. But he can't hide forever. She must be worried sick.

When I walk into the kitchen, carrying my book and Radford's, I'm shocked to see Nora dicing a chilled heart into cubes. "What are you doing?" I ask. "Who was that?"

"Another of Porky's cousins," she replies. "Hardly any of the vamps eat solid food, and those few who do barely remember what anything tastes like. I hope."

I'm embarrassed for doubting her—Nora, of all people, who has more faith in me than I deserve. I wonder in how many small ways she's circumvented Radford.

A phone rings, and it takes me a second to realize it's Nora's.

She holds up one finger. "Freddy! No? Really. Oh, no. Not at all. If the master has other ideas . . ." The chef ends the call. "Change of menu. I'm supposed to just whip up—"

"Nora," I whisper, urgent. "Radford is planning to serve up staffers to the partygoers tonight. He's going to order the guests to drain their own PAs."

She sets down the dicing knife. "What are you asking of me, hon?"

"Warn them, so they can run or fight or—"

"It wouldn't help," she says in a low voice. "They're in love with their masters or with the idea of being turned. They'd never believe what's coming, and they'd report us for treason. I'm in enough trouble as it is."

I should've anticipated that. "If we can create a distraction, I'll—"

"You'll what?" she whispers, incredulous. "*Destroy* Dracula?"

"Yes," I say, without hesitation, "and you and your son will finally be safe."

I project confidence. I project competence. I wow my crowd.

I beat Father to the parlor just barely in time to set *Curse of the Cubs* on his end table, plop in a decorative way on the rug, and open my acting book.

"Evening, sugar," Radford says, entering in a tux. "Why, what's this?" He sets the kukri knife on the arm of his recliner and picks up the book.

By the standard that applies, it's not much of a gift.

"Merely a token," I assure him. "I thought..." I thought *what*? "Perhaps in celebration of your death-day we could"—I've got it!—"attend the Country Music Awards. I'll arrange for front-row seats."

At this, he begins to tear up, momentarily speechless.

As I leaf through my book, trying to strategize, Harrison escorts Zachary into the parlor. I make sure my glance seems unconcerned. I don't detect any bruises, cuts, contusions, punctures, or broken bones.

I'm ashamed of the way I treated him at the Edison. I hope he doesn't hate me, but I can't apologize or explain, not now. I have to maintain my façade.

Zachary

WHEN HARRISON AND I ARRIVE, my gaze goes first to Miranda.

She's studying *Wow the Crowd.* She's dressed in a bridal, full-length, diamond-studded sky-blue gown. She's wearing a thick black ribbon around her neck. Her dark hair is curled in ringlets. Black lipstick. Pale pink blush. Pale pink eye shadow. No jewelry. Her shoes look like ballet slippers. They peek out from the skirt. She sits with her legs tucked on the werebear rug in front of the fireplace.

"Miranda?" I say.

Ignoring me, she wets a dainty fingertip and turns a page.

Drac's feet are up on the La-Z-Boy recliner. He's sharpening the knife that was a gift from Sabine and Philippe. *Curse of the Cubs* is on the table beside him. His jacket is draped over the back of the Arts-and-Crafts sofa to his right.

If Michael hadn't yanked my powers, I could use my radiance. Light up like a supernova and take Drac out.

Except that Miranda also would be directly exposed.

I can't bring myself to give up on my girl. Not yet. Besides, if my theory holds, Harrison may be redeemable, too.

If only I had a sword of divine flame like Michael's.

Harrison's cell rings. He takes the call, excuses himself, and then reappears. "Presenting Sabine, Philippe, and Geoff."

It's Geoff Calvo, Miranda's high-school crush. He's dressed in formalwear. He's showing off fangs. We're talking date to the princess. Everything but the corsage.

For the kid to have already transformed, they must've fed him the blood and killed him not long after he left here.

I was jealous of Calvo. I admit it. But what a waste! He was so young.

Miranda smiles like the Mona Lisa, but I'd swear I catch a glimpse of horror in her eyes. I don't trust it, though. My girl was never this good of an actress.

Sabine curtsies to Drac and then Miranda, gesturing to Calvo. "The master informed us that you would reconsider him as a consort."

Miranda stands. She smoothes her skirt. She extends her hand for Calvo to kiss.

"Dear boy," Drac begins, acknowledging Calvo's bow, "we have a surprise for you tonight. This . . ."—he gestures my way—"is Her Highness's former personal assistant. He has been discharged. In honor of your introduction to eternal society, I invite you to take the first bite."

Had I felt badly for Calvo? He's at my throat in an instant. I have no time to struggle. His teeth tear my skin, worm into my vein. Pain flashes. Invasive. Intoxicating.

Before I know it, I'm numb. Is this death? It must be. As if from a distance, I hear Drac's voice again. I'm going to hell, I realize. And this is the welcoming committee.

Miranda

IT HAPPENS IN A BLUR. Geoff latches onto Zachary's neck. Meanwhile, Radford is saying, "Never fear, sugar plum. You're welcome to finish the traitor off."

I'm ready to tear Zachary free when the neophyte vampire shoves him aside.

I'm not sure what's wrong. Geoff's lips are blistered. They're swollen, burned, no, burning? As he raises his hands to his face, I realize his cheeks are on fire. He takes a drunken step. Flames spread to his throat, eating away the flesh.

How is this possible? I'm as repulsed as I am mesmerized.

The neck folds. The head separates. One knee cracks on the way down.

The fire consumes him. It feels like Texas in July.

All that's left of Geoff are scorch marks on the rug.

The boy I spent so long pining for is completely gone.

I'm not glad of that. Nothing here tonight makes me happy, but it's a relief that he won't be corrupted any further and that he won't hurt anyone else.

Sabine and Philippe trade a look of alarm. Harrison pours a glass of blood wine from a crystal decanter and hands it to Radford. Then the eternal PA takes a shot straight from the mouth of the decanter himself.

It was the blood, I realize, Zachary's blood. "What was that, a protection spell?" I ask him. "What are you? A sorcerer, warlock, Hogwarts grad? *What?*"

He says the most ludicrous thing. "I'm on a mission from God."

Even stranger? The answer seems to make sense to Radford. He raises his glass in a toast to Zachary. "You," he muses. "It was you. You know, I chose her because of you. I meant to adopt the other one. Then you appeared in the moonlight, and I took refuge in the deepest shadows, delighted by my good fortune. When you, of all beings, appeared to her, I knew that she must be special. I had to make her mine."

I turn to Radford. "What is he, Father? What do you mean?"

He sighs. "They just don't make angels of the Lord the way they used to."

It's like I've been punched in the heart. I remember Zachary asking me at the bookstore if I believed in angels. I remember the tattoo on his chest. I . . .

Oh, my God. It's true.

I asked when we first met if he was a wereperson. I instinctively knew that he wasn't human. No human could have such silken hair and flawless skin. No human could eat like a sumo wrestler, never work out, and look like that.

The love and lust of my life is as holy as I'm unholy. No wonder Zachary kept rejecting me! I'm positive that sucking face with a bloodsucker falls in the Thou Shalt Not category. Why is he here? Shouldn't he be topping a Christmas tree or decorating an Italian fresco or singing in a choir or strumming a harp or, I don't know, molting?

Where are his wings?

"An angel," I breathe, finally able to form words again.

"A fallen one, apparently," Radford observes. "Likely of the guardian variety."

Sabine excuses herself to freshen up, and Philippe exits with her. They don't ask or wait for permission. They just go.

"How do you know that he's fallen?" Harrison asks.

Radford laughs. "Fully endowed angels don't tend to spend quality time with eternals. Even daughter-seducing do-gooders like this one. Besides, if he weren't fallen, he would've already vanished in a twinkling or used his radiance to vaporize us all."

"He's a guardian angel?" I ask, trying to make sense of it.

That's when Zachary speaks. "Yeah. I am, or at least I was, yours."

Miranda

"REMOVE THIS to the main courtyard," Radford orders Harrison, slipping on his jacket. "He'll make fine entertainment."

"You can't kill me," Zachary says as blood wells at his neck wound.

Radford's smile darkens the room. "I know. It makes you the perfect, perpetual victim. I can only imagine how publicly torturing you, night after night, year after year, over the centuries will enhance my reputation."

It takes all of my will power not to visibly react to that.

As Harrison leads Zachary out of the parlor, Radford pulls a cigar from his inside breast pocket and calls after them. "Wait. I'll go with you. I have the most jim-dandy idea." He turns to me. "Sugar?"

"With your permission, Father, I'll meet you at the gala." I must act now, while he's preoccupied. He may be able to travel as dust and mist, but he can't be two places at once. It's the most logical explanation for his not foiling the dungeon breakout. He was distracted either by observing me or by Harrison's return. "I wish to speak to Sabine privately about . . ." I settle on the safest default I can muster, at least when addressing an undead southern gentleman. "Um, it's girl talk."

When I find Sabine standing alone in a third-floor hallway, she's sipping blood from a monogrammed silver hip-flask and staring out the window overlooking the central courtyard. Apparently, I'm not the only one who likes to know where the vampire king is.

"You are dismayed, princess?" Sabine asks as I approach. "Please understand. You said one thing about Geoff, but then your Father called —"

"I know," I reply. "You couldn't defy the master. Sucks, doesn't it?"

"I beg your pardon?" she asks, raising a curtain of mascara-laden eyelashes.

I can hardly believe her corseted mermaid dress. Sabine takes her fashion as seriously as her feminism, yet tonight she looks like a vapid doll because that's the expectation. Radford's expectation. She has to hate it.

"Sabine, may I have a word with you in confidence?"

She bows as well as she can with the sewn-in waist.

"I feel I should warn you." It's a baby step, nothing Radford wouldn't excuse should he catch word of it. "Tonight the master will order his subjects to dine on their own personal assistants. It's to send a message after some glitches in the management of the royal staff. Should you wish to protect your—"

"'Glitches' like employing and daring to torture an angel? *Mon Dieu!*"

Jackpot. I see no need to clarify that I'm the one who hired said angel in the first place. Sabine trembles, likely recalling the fallout of her handmaiden's indiscretion, the indignity of having to eat the nun's body herself, the fire that ripped away Philippe's good looks and their long-time home. I bet she's thinking that payback for angel abuse—that divine retribution—is far greater than she can endure.

"When we met, I was taken by his sophistication," she says, referring to Radford, "his unusual respect for women, as an eternal male of his seniority. That he would name a young woman as his heir is significant. However, the master is no Old Blood."

He's no Old Blood, but she is. She's among their most admired and feared.

I suspect that at one time she imagined herself in my blue slippers, as the dragon princess, if not as queen.

The implication of her words constitutes treason. It's brave of her to direct them at me, Dracula's daughter.

"They say," Sabine adds, "as he prematurely heightens his abilities through magic, he loses his mind."

"It's true," I reply. "I'm his favorite." I untie the black ribbon around my neck to reveal the scabbed knife wound. "And look."

Sabine's hand flies to her throat.

Sabine, who once chose damnation over the guillotine.

It hasn't been long since her actions placed her temporarily outside Radford's good graces. I tell her about the fire in my bedroom, and I can almost hear her wondering about the one in the Latin Quarter. I wouldn't be surprised if Radford had ordered it set.

"His affection for you," she says. "It is now an obsession."

It works to my advantage that I showed her mercy when he likely wouldn't have. Sabine holds up a finger, glancing again at the courtyard scene below.

"There are rumbles among the aristocracy," she adds in a soft voice. "It did not help that the master never appeared on his international tour. His media manipulations may have fooled the middle class, the peasants. The elite, we know. His instability puts the Mantle at risk. It is a dangerous time, princess—not only for the royal family

267 ⌒

but for the aristocracy as well. Of late, across the continents, we are more and more questioned, more and more dismissed by the gentry, even the common citizenry. Just over a year ago, the entire Southwest U.S. aristocracy was destroyed in a series of bombing attacks."

Almost there. "The master can't even rule his own castle," I agree, "let alone the underworld. It must be done. Tonight at the party. We'll catch him off-guard."

Sabine raises her small chin. "You are doing this for the angel."

I don't deny it. "Not only for Zachary, but, yes, he is part of it."

"You love him."

Sabine may be wicked, but she understands love.

"Help me," I say, "and you will be rewarded. I am the rightful heir. I can facilitate the smoothest transition."

"I like you, princess. I do. But we are beings of self-interest, not of honor."

I don't blame her for doubting me. I play a card I have no right to. "I'm not only giving you my word, Sabine. I'm giving you the word of my angel, too."

She audibly gasps. "The word of God?"

It's blasphemous to agree. For all I know, doing so may cause me to burst into flames. Hopefully, though, He will forgive me this, if nothing more. "Yes."

Zachary

I'M CHAINED FLAT ON MY BACK to the thirty-foot-long buffet table in the middle of the courtyard. I can't believe this is happening. I've never felt so helpless, stupid, or ridiculous in my entire life. It was one thing to have thought I was a fallen angel. Another to hear from Joshua that I've only "slipped." But being laid out as the decorative centerpiece of The Dracula's social high point must go down in the history of heaven as the single most revolting performance by an angel of the order guardian.

As Harrison unbuttons my shirt, I spit in his face.

"I like it," his brother, Freddy, says. He backs away, positioning his hands like a movie director trying to figure

269 ᦡᦞ

out the camera shot. "I like the drama, the composition. An angel, you say?"

"A fallen angel." Harrison scowls as he wipes his cheek.

"Foolish, fallen angel," Drac proclaims, puffing on his stogie. He slams the kukri knife into the wood, through the light-blue tablecloth, alongside my temple. "Don't you know you're supposed to have changed sides?"

Where is Miranda? I wonder. Where?

"The first guests are parking in the west lot," Harrison announces.

At that, Drac dissolves into mist.

Freddy flips open his cell and talks as he walks the perimeter of the setup.

Harrison risks leaning over me, back into spitting range. "I knew you were too good-looking to be human." His voice drops. "I didn't know there were angels."

I may have failed with Miranda. But I give the pitch another try. "You knew firsthand about the demonic. Why wouldn't you believe in us?"

"We were raised in this world, Freddy and I, children of servants who were children of servants for generations. It's all we've known."

I'm buying that only up to a point. "Your brother doesn't want to vamp out."

"No," Harrison agrees. "He would've run from this life long ago . . ."

"If it weren't for you." That's what I figured. That whole Hannibal-Lecter-party-planner shtick might fool the vamps. Not me. "It's not too late," I tell Harrison, hoping I'm right. "You can still make a choice for good."

Before Harrison can reply, Freddy rejoins the conversation.

"You're lucky that this one showed up, Harrison," he says. "The master's original plan for tonight was to put *you* in the holy-water dunking tank."

Harrison nods absently. "You have a little angel tattooed on your chest," he tells me, like I don't know that. "A cherub."

Freddy pushes up his wire-frame glasses. I almost swallow my tongue when he says, "That is not one of the *cherubim*. That is a fat, naked white baby with wings."

Where did I hear that before? Joshua. Amtrak.

It's no coincidence. It's what? Divine nudging, I suppose.

Freddy is a human being. He has a guardian angel. Freddy, Nora, all of the human servants scheduled to be killed. Their angels must be doing what I used to. Indirectly encouraging, inspiring. Pulling strings.

Even if Miranda has deserted me, I'm not alone in this. I remember what Josh said at the museum. Heaven is on my side.

"Speaking of the fallen," Freddy adds, "oh, brother of mine . . ."

"Not now," Harrison says, walking off. "There are guests to greet."

"What's going to happen next?" I ask.

Freddy begins tossing blue and white rose petals on me. Artfully. "Well, we're going BYOB since the party favors are AWOL. The resulting kitsch factor at a royal gala is in itself something, but it's not that nifty. So, the idea is to cut out your heart, the heart of an angel, and exhibit it around on a silver platter. The guests will be warned not to taste but invited to stab it with their lobster forks."

"You're going to do that?" I ask Freddy. "Cut out my heart?"

When we first met, I would've believed it of him in, well, a heartbeat. But since then I've been getting a much more complicated vibe.

"Oh, no," he clarifies, working the blade of the knife free. "The master is reserving that honor for the princess."

Miranda

I TWIRL THROUGH THE GALA, biding time, until Sabine moves to my side beneath the south wall overhang.

"Philippe has seen to the sentries," she says. "Only three are left. They are taking a little nap."

I know this isn't Sabine and Philippe's first coup d'état, but I'm still impressed. "The crowd?"

"The local aristocracy is more loyal to the master than the international set is, but they are survivors. They will gauge the situation. Even if most of the domestic eternals stand with Radford, we will not be without support."

An underworld war. Sabine speaks English fluently, but her accent is noticeably thicker. She's nervous, too.

"Be ready," I tell her, turning the kukri knife. "Philippe, too."

She raises a large brass goblet as if to toast me, but doesn't drink.

Later, at the buffet, I don't have time to say anything to Zachary. He can't see me because of the blue silk blindfold. He can't say anything because of the matching gag.

Radford appears immediately by my side.

The hilt of the knife I'm holding is cold to my touch and at times seems to vibrate slightly. Or maybe that's my hand shaking.

It might seem ill advised, Radford's decision to have the knife placed in my hands. Yet he's always surrounded himself with deadly materials—the weapons throughout the castle, the fire of the torches and candles, the holy water in the reflecting pool. Furthermore, he's yet to let his gaze stray from the blade while I'm within striking range.

Harrison rings his handbell, calling the attention of all assembled. As befitting their seniority, Sabine and Philippe flank us. She to Radford's right, he to my left.

Once the crowd quiets, Harrison announces, "Tonight it is the great pleasure of The Dracula, exalted master of eternals, king and ruler of the Mantle of Dracul, to present for public torture and humiliation an angel of the Lord."

The crowd shrinks back. A few raise their faces to the

heavens. Some stare at Zachary like he's a sideshow freak. Others stare at Radford in awe.

He booms, "Understand that your master is no fool. I know there are those among you who have doubted my capacity to rule. Yet I present to you the desecration of a holy being. No mere human devotee of the enemy, but one who foils our efforts on a universal scale. He is an angel fallen—stripped of flight and radiance—but still in the service of the opposition."

Zachary protests against the gag, struggles against the chains.

"Sugar," Radford prompts.

I've been improvising as I've gone along, but now I don't know what to do next and I've run out of time. I raise the kukri knife in both hands high over my head as if to plunge it into Zachary's heart. I'd meant to stab Radford instead, but my positioning is wrong. The master vampire is too attentive.

For the first time since I died, I close my eyes and pray.

"One moment, Your Highness! Excuse me. Coming through." Freddy steps in front of the onlookers to record the moment on video. "Look this way! Exalted Master, Princess Cutie." He pans. "Frenchies?"

Even under the circumstances, I can't help being amused.

Freddy gets away with the attitude because he's the best at what he does, and Radford insists on having the best. He demanded the finest effort of his "princess" from the beginning, and tonight that's what he's finally going to get.

Freddy adjusts his focus. "That's fantastic! Carry on!"

The lure of preening for the camera distracts Radford. I take one last look at him, my murderer, the monster who ripped me from everyone I loved, the one who stole my future and reinvented me for his own wicked purposes.

He's handsome, distinguished-looking, there's no denying it. But those *GQ* looks and the royal posturing, they're a lie. I'm sick of lies. I'm sick of this whole existence.

I take a half step closer to Philippe, tighten my grip on the knife, and bring the blade down at an angle, driving it through the tux and into Radford's abdomen.

It's not a killing blow. But if I'd tried to turn and strike upward through the heart, he would've blocked me.

Radford reaches out, his hand breaking the scab around my neck.

This is it, I realize, the moment I find out whether my alliances hold.

And then Sabine tosses the contents of her goblet into Radford's face. He lets go of me with a piercing cry, covering his burning skin with his hands, only to burn his palms, too. Holy water, I realize. The knife is still firmly lodged, bleeding him out, as he staggers backward and falls to his knees.

Victor—he of the baby-teeth necklace—is next up, rushing to his master's defense, only to be blasted by an electric charge from Philippe's bat-head cane.

Elina leaps over the buffet table to land in front of me. She pauses just long enough to show off her forked tongue. It's all I can do to dodge the attack when Sabine steps between us, knocking out Elina's fangs with one punch.

As for me, I have powers but no clue about hand-to-hand combat. It was one subject Radford overlooked in my training.

I'm the only one of my kind, though, who seems to have that problem. The courtyard has become a frenzied battle zone. Vampires are skittering up and down the walls like scorpions, leaping into battle. Three in wolf form collide in the middle, a blur of flying fur and dripping jaws.

Freddy and Nora shout to the human PAs, food servers, and the harpist, herding them out of the way, out of the fray, through the castle to safety.

The parking lot will empty fast.

And Radford? He lies, twisting on the courtyard's stone floor. His forearms cover his face like a shield. He's wounded, weakened, but still lethal.

Zachary

PHILIPPE TEARS APART the chains and helps me down from the table. I rip off the blindfold. Spit out the gag. Both of my legs are asleep from the hips down. They buckle.

"Easy, *monsieur*," Philippe says. "Take my arm."

"You're not an evil vampire?" I ask.

His tone is friendly. "We are all evil vampires," he says. "But some of us are on your side. I would ask forgiveness for me and Sabine, but it is too late for us, *non*?"

"Not my department," I say. "But I'll put in a good word."

I don't know where Drac is, and I don't care. Once I get enough circulation to stand, I take Miranda's arm. "Your throat!" I exclaim. "You're bleeding!"

Miranda grabs several light-blue napkins and presses them against the wound. "It's not deep," she says, "and I heal fast, much faster than a human. I'll be fine."

I press my lips to her dark hair. "You're sure?"

I still don't know if she's redeemable, but for just a moment it matters less.

Miranda gives me a brisk kiss on the lips. "We'll talk later."

"Hang on," I say, but she's so fast. In a flash, I lose sight of her in the crowd.

Frustrated, I take in the larger scene. The party has turned into pandemonium. A fury of fiends. Tables and chairs are flying. One vamp after another stumbles or is tossed into a reflecting pool, where they're vaporized.

Philippe's bat-head cane shoots out an electric charge, blasting an incoming wolf-form attacker.

I'm knocked to the ground by a vamp who keeps on going. Standing, I'm smacked down again by a stray elbow.

At first I can't tell who's winning. I can't even tell who's on whose side. I'm not even sure the combatants know or if they're just creating carnage for the fun of it. Based on the curses being thrown around, though, it looks like the majority back Miranda. Or at least Sabine.

I'm on my feet when three werebears burst into the courtyard.

Brenek has returned; he's brought along Mama and Papa Bear, and man, are they pissed! Did I mention that Brenek is a big guy? Turns out he's not even full grown. His parents look supersize.

Immense claws rip through undead skin. They tear off heads and limbs.

Only problem? They're not fighting on anybody's side. They're lashing out at any vampire they can reach.

"Miranda!" I don't see her anywhere. "Miranda!"

Something falls from the sky and breaks on my head. I'm drenched.

I duck a flying armless body and spot more black balloons raining down.

On the rooftop of the castle—it's the dungeon escapees. A handful of them anyway. Maybe ten, sporting street clothes. The ones in good enough shape to fight.

To my left, Freddy is in trouble. He draws a stake from his inside jacket pocket, and a snarling female vamp bats it away. Before I can move to help him, a balloon explodes against the attacker, dousing her. She shrieks and crumbles, smoking.

Like the pool, I realize, the balloons are filled with holy water.

Freddy takes advantage of the moment to grab a nearby torch.

Another vamp wails—loud and furious—as a balloon finds its target.

"Miranda!" In the chaos, I can barely hear myself. "Miranda!"

Across the courtyard, a fiend grabs Nora and bends her neck.

In midair, I fling the punch bowl at the monster's lower back. The force of it sends both him and Nora tumbling. I just manage to catch her. Rise with her in my arms.

I'm flying! Flying. It's a miracle.

"Good Lord, boy!" Nora exclaims. "What are you? A werepelican?"

I guess she missed Drac's announcement.

When I don't reply, Nora is quiet a moment. Then she exclaims, "Oh, my God!"

"Closer," I say, setting her down on the roof and taking flight again.

She's not the only one who's noticed. Vamps below catch sight of me. My wings.

I'd acted on reflex, and there they were. I don't know if this means I'm reinstated. But it has to be a good sign, right?

Unless I just blew it again by accidentally *showing* my wings in a courtyard largely filled with denizens of hell. That would be my luck.

I don't think so, though. It's not just my wings that are

back. Once again, I can feel the power to radiate heaven's light. It's singing through my body.

Like in the Dallas cemetery, it would be so easy to shine.

But no. Not here. Not now. Not with Miranda in the open like that.

Still, I scan the crowd. Do they know what my radiance could do to them? At least some of them do. A sultry brunette morphs into a bat and bails. Others cower. Two of those in wolf form change back.

The balloon attack stops.

Freddy raises his torch.

Mama Bear and Papa Bear and Brenek rear up on their hind legs and roar.

Miranda

RADFORD'S SHAPE CHANGES, blurs. The tux melts away. He lifts his head, showing a raw, hairless, wolf-form face. His skin looks like lava. Meat hangs off the bones.

Sabine knew how to hurt him.

This isn't like the lovely *whoosh* of the holy-water pool.

"Sugar," he growls, staggering to his feet. In his anguish, there's no pretense. The southern accent is thick. "Traitor!"

He writhes, his face a man's again. A fang falls from the disintegrating gums. His torso goes lupine. He bends, gasping. Tiny, useless bat wings spring from his shoulder blades. He yanks the knife from his chest but doesn't have the fingers to hang on to it.

The weapon falls with a clack onto the stone. I take a step toward it, and Radford opens his mouth, spewing a cloud of smoke that smells like hell.

"Princess!" It's Harrison, holding up my battle-axe.

He tosses it my way, and my preternatural reflexes allow me a one-handed catch.

I charge Radford's flailing form, swing the weapon, and end so much suffering. His head falls from his body and rolls into oblivion. The body disintegrates, too.

It's not showy, like what happened to Geoff. The pieces simply turn to ash.

The crowd is silent. I count half a dozen motionless bodies on the ground, some dismembered. I have no idea if any of the dead were human. Sabine's skirt is torn and her lip is cut, but she looks satisfied. Philippe is hardly ruffled.

I glance up, and there he is, Zachary, his wings— *wings* —strong in the cool wind.

I remember illustrations in the Bible in which an angel appears with light shooting from his halo. Zachary doesn't have a halo. His body isn't glowing.

A glimmer of light is there, though. It's in the way he looks at me.

The way we're looking at each other.

Some in the crowd follow my gaze and gesture to the rest. They're staring back and forth between us, as if we're players in an unearthly tennis match.

The Bears lower their heads.

Whoever's on the roof, they've joined hands and raised them high.

A few vampires try to shield themselves. Others flee on two legs or four. Penelope crouches, hissing low. Victor rips off his baby-teeth necklace and begins to cry.

The majority inch toward me, for protection.

My audience is shaken, receptive. At least tonight, they won't question my youth or raise challenge. I step forward, plant my dress slippers on the ash, and raise my voice. "I hereby claim the Mantle of Dracul." I pause, awaiting a reaction.

Nobody's arguing. Is that it? Sabine said that would do it.

Should I say something else regal to sort of seal the deal? I'm at a loss. Then Sabine curtsies, Philippe bows, and all of the assembled undead follow their example.

"Your Exalted Majesty," Harrison calls, walking toward me, "there's a DustBuster in the cabinet in the storage closet off the kitchen. With your permission, I'll fetch it, clean up that"—he gestures toward what had been his master—"mess for you, and dispose of the ashes in the reflecting pool."

Vicious fellow, but you have to love him. "Of course," I agree. "Please do."

When he reaches my side, I say, "Thanks" under my breath.

Harrison straightens his spine and his bow tie. "My pleasure, Your Majesty," he says with a wink. "It's apparently the only sort of thing I'm good for around here."

The party resumes as if the battle never happened. As the Bears and rooftop warriors retreat, Zachary, still airborne, announces to all that they're under his protection. Human servants, those who survived and decided to stick around, clear the bodies. Freddy administers first aid to anyone with a pulse who isn't badly hurt. Nora coordinates hospital runs for the more seriously wounded.

By undead standards, it's the best party in centuries.

My angel descends. He takes my hands in his. "What the hell just happened?"

"I'm the scariest vampire in the world," I reply. "I'm the new Dracula."

Zachary

I PERSONALLY ESCORT the Bears and the holy-balloon bombers (as they're calling themselves) through the subdivision to a couple of parked minivans. I'm relieved to have them out of harm's way.

Along the way, no one says much. They're pretty starstruck, though I've ditched the wings. After the humans are loaded, the Bears shift back. It looks painful and smells like an evergreen forest on steroids. We all do a bang-up job of pretending that the fact that they end up naked is no big deal.

As the Bears throw on long cloaks, Brenek quickly fills me in on the prisoners' escape—minor injuries but zero fatalities on our side. It's the best news I've heard in ages. As for the sentries, Brenek tore off one of their heads himself. The flamethrowers took out two more, and he's not sure about the rest. I wonder how Delta fared.

"If you ever need anything . . ." Brenek offers his large hand, and I shake it with both of mine. "Seriously," he adds. "Standing offer."

"All the kids are safe," Papa Bear assures me. "We made sure everyone who needs medical treatment is receiving it. The rest are at the house with my brothers."

I hand him Father Ramos's business card. "This man should be able to help get everybody home." I remember what Miranda said about how some of the prisoners were from worse places or had been sold by their parents or pimps. "Or someplace better."

"Thank you," Mama Bear says. A substantial woman at six foot five, she explains that the local Bear community had been searching nonstop for Brenek. It had been weeks. They'd begun to lose hope. Her words dissolve into sobs. She puts aside her awe to hug me.

Once the taillights fade in the distance, I try to change myself to ethereal form, planning to reappear back in the castle. It doesn't work.

I focus more fully. Still no luck.

Flight and radiance may have been returned to me. But all is not forgiven.

I'm still stuck on the mortal plane.

I find Miranda with Philippe in her office. She's seated behind the massive metal desk, and he's perched in the chair across from her.

I'll never forget tonight. Miranda—a girl who as a human cowered before standard-issue high-school divas and didn't have the strength to climb the rope in Gym, claiming the worldwide throne of the undead.

On one hand, I'm proud of her. On the other, I'm mortified. Why the hell would she want the Mantle of Dracul?

As I walk in, Miranda picks up the kukri knife. Slices her right palm open.

"What are you doing?" I exclaim.

She winces. Squeezes her hand into a fist. Urges the dripping blood into an inkwell. Then she dips in a pen and scribbles something.

Still ignoring me, Miranda turns the paper toward Philippe and gives him the quill. After he makes a notation, she picks up a brass ink stamp, wets it on a pad, and with a small thud pounds it against the page.

In a businesslike voice she says, "If you track down Harrison, he'll make and file the requisite number of copies."

Philippe struggles to stand. Reaches for his bat-head cane. "*Merci*, princess."

She begins, "I'm not—"

But he waves his hand. "I speak for myself and Sabine

when we beg to disagree." Philippe offers a deferential nod to me on his way out.

Once the door closes, I can't keep my mouth shut. "What are you thinking? Taking out Drac—kudos on that. Really. But is *this* why you did it? So you could become the biggest, baddest vamp of them all?"

Miranda extends her nails and raps them on the metal desk. "You say you were my guardian angel. Does that mean you watched me *all* the time? Like when I got my period or doctored a zit or took a shower or—"

"I'm an angel, not a Peeping Tom." I can't meet her eyes. Shower time was one of my favorites. "I knew what I was doing then." It's a bald-faced lie. If I'd known what I was doing, we'd never have been in this situation in the first place.

Suddenly, I know why I'm still incapable of becoming ethereal. As glad as I am to have seen Drac bite it, I'm not the one who fulfilled the mission of the Big Boss. It was Miranda who beheaded the monster.

Heaven's gates are closed to me forever.

Miranda

"AND I KNOW what I'm doing now!" Did I actually say that? "Biggest, baddest vamp of them all. Is that what you think of me?"

"I . . ." It's not his best comeback.

I need a drink. I walk to the reception area. The glass of blood wine tastes too good. It's a human blend. Radford must've changed it during his brief reemergence. "I'm not The Dracula, not anymore. I just abdicated the Mantle to Sabine. Philippe signed the decree as my witness."

"Oh." Zachary says, looking appropriately chastened. "Sorry." It takes him a moment to regroup. "Why have a Dracula at all?"

The good can be so simple. "Until the last vampire fades away, The Dracula is necessary for order. If there is a power vacuum, there'll be an undead free-for-all. Our laws and traditions don't exist without reason. Ultimately, they protect the humans as much as they do us."

"Until the last vampire fades away," he murmurs, likely wishing this was that night. "You're sure about this?"

I let the blood play on my tongue. "Yes and no."

Part of me is relieved when Zachary takes the glass. Part of me wants to tear his throat out for it. Thank God I can't drink him.

I'm thinking how unworthy I am when he falls to his knees. "I have to tell you something," he says, and my first thought is ludicrous—that he's proposing marriage.

Instead, he offers me the most extraordinary story about the night I died.

Call me naive, but it never occurred to me that my abduction and murder had been planned. I never thought to question what Radford was doing in the cemetery.

He meant to kill Lucy. He used Kurt, an undercover undead DVD rental guy, to identify her and lure her out that night. Why? Because she thought bad boys in black leather were sexy? Because she liked scary movies and chatting online with her fandom buddies?

Because, I realize, thinking back to the old photo from the feature story, she was the living image of Radford's human daughters.

In all the years he was a vampire, Radford never stopped mourning his life. *That girl who was in the dungeon and looks like Lucy, the one I couldn't drink . . . She must've been a near miss, a discarded candidate for princess.*

I think of all the girls who have died over the centuries. Who knows how many of us have been snuffed out since the reign of Dracula Prime.

Not Lucy, though. She's alive even though she was specifically targeted by—as Zachary would say—the biggest and baddest of vamps. How miraculous is that?

Zachary

MY GIRL OFFERS ME THE HEALTHIEST, most wholly human smile I've ever seen. "Thank you, thank you."

She's cracked. I've pushed her over the edge.

"Do you understand what I'm saying?" I ask, standing.

"Yes!" Miranda leaps to hug me. She kisses my right cheek, my left, and the tip of my nose. "You saved Lucy. She's my best friend, the only close friend I had before you."

It's amazing. Inspiring. I didn't know any vampire could think that way. Few humans would be so selfless.

I'm still a work-in-progress myself.

I've wondered why vampires still exist. Why the archangels weren't asked to wipe them out a long time ago. Michael alone could level an army of the undead. But if some of them, if *any* of them, are like Miranda—soul and salvation still in play, maybe the reason is as simple and astounding as that.

Whatever my girl is, whatever she's done, how could the Big Boss reject her?

How can I? I'm tempted to suggest a visit to the four-poster bed in my second-floor quarters. Right now, I'm aching for all of her passion, even the demonic.

I have to remember, though, that she's still a teenager. We've hardly more than kissed. The upside is that we'll both walk the earth for centuries.

Walk away from this foul place. Find solace somewhere in the shadows between good and evil. Make love until the End Days.

Miranda

ZACHARY SAYS THE NICEST THING. "I missed you this week."

I wonder if I've drunk enough blood to blush. "I'm sorry I fired you."

I mean it. I do. The words sound funny, though, out loud. Before I know it, we're both laughing, and Zachary's dipping in for a kiss.

If I start touching him, I'll lose my courage in the pleasure. "I still have something to do tonight. Why don't you clean up? Meet me in the central courtyard in ten minutes?"

I need to center myself. I have to remember that Zachary is a holy being. I don't deserve his love or touch. I don't deserve to go on. I can't go on like this.

The last lines of *A Tale of Two Cities* come back to me: "It is a far, far better thing that I do, than I have ever done; it is a far, far better rest that I go to than I have ever known."

My English teacher would approve, but I have to find my own words to explain to Zachary what must be done. Tonight is our last.

Missing Miranda

Zachsgirl

What a cool blog! I'm wowed by how much time you've put into it.

It looks to me like you're the BEST best friend in the world.

Maybe you should visit Miranda's house sometimes and play with Mr. Nesbit. I bet her mom wouldn't mind. She might even let you bring him home and take care of him.

I'm sure that if Miranda ever surfed by, she'd want to say thanks for everything. She'd want to tell you that she loves you and wants you to be happy and to enjoy the blessings of life.

This time, I press SEND.

Miranda

THE WRECKAGE FROM THE PARTY has been cleared. The stone has been hosed down.

I could order the reflecting pool refilled with holy water, but the longer I wait, the more likely I am to lose my nerve. I hear my angel's footsteps, drawing closer to where I've seated myself on the foot-high rock border wall.

"It's empty," I say.

Zachary solves the mystery. "After Harrison dumped Drac's remains, he drained it. Said it was a health hazard."

Harrison would say that.

Zachary offers his hand, and I take it, rising.

"What's your pleasure?" he asks.

I'm surprised by the invitation in his words and tone. I realize he's somehow convinced himself that we could have a future. It's the biggest compliment anyone's ever given me. I only wish it were true. "I have a favor to ask. Two actually."

He doesn't hesitate. "Anything for you."

We walk, hand in hand, to the middle of the castle courtyard. The horizon has lightened. The stars have faded. We're moments from a new day.

"You're stuck on earth, right?"

"I used to think so." His smile is wry. "That I was stuck. Now, there's nowhere else I'd rather be."

I shut my eyes against the pain I'm about to cause. "Guardian angels help people?"

"We try," he says. "There are limits. But yeah, we do our best."

I rest my palm over his heart, noticing the Band-Aid covering his neck wound. "I wonder if you could help vampires like me, if they're not too far gone." When Zachary hesitates, I press, "Isn't that what you've been doing here, trying to help?"

He brushes stray hair from my face. "You could say that."

It's a burden, a duty, more than I have the right to ask. Still, I know he loves me. Is there a difference between love and duty? I haven't walked on this earth long, but

I don't think so. Love isn't only passion and joy. It's also sacrifice.

"So will you?" I press. "Will you try to save other vampires?"

Zachary doesn't take long to answer. "It's not all up to me," he says with a meaningful glance upward. "And ultimately, each will have to decide their fate for themselves. But I'll do what I can."

Before I can thank him, his lips send a surge of energy into my body. The fact that I'm the least vampy vamp in vamp history? It doesn't matter. In that moment, I'm all girl, ravenous, desperate for more. I let my hands roam, searching, discovering.

I'm tempted to take what pleasure I can, here on the rock, as the sun breaks through the darkness, as spring pushes away winter, as heaven sings down.

If Zachary keeps me, if he loses himself inside me, in my body and my love, though, he'll be a lost cause, too. Truly fallen, eternally damned. I can't let that happen, even if it means we could stay together, even if his touch humbles me, humanizes me, and despite the ecclesiastical stakes, makes me long to tie him to the wall in classic Dracul fashion and lick him like a Bomb Pop. "You shouldn't do that."

"What?" he asks. "Touch you?"

"About the other favor," I say, removing myself from his arms. "I can't be this thing anymore."

He doesn't understand. "We'll take it one night—"

"No." I say it fast. "I mean, it *ends* tonight, this excuse for an existence. The blood by moonlight, the power through intimidation, the trafficking in innocents, the lost conscience, lost self." I let the words "lost soul" remain unsaid. "I need—"

"Suicide is—"

"Not what we're talking about." I knew he would fight me. Yet I can't leave him without a good-bye, an explanation. I hate this, but he has to understand. He has to. "What I did tonight to Radford, was that murder?"

"No. No, it wasn't. But why can't you—"

"I'm walking, I'm talking, but Zachary . . . I'm dead. I have been for quite a while. To borrow an expression from Grandma Peggy, it's high time I started acting like it."

He shakes his head. "You're not that . . . I mean—"

"Please understand. This is my chance to die as some remnant of the girl I was, not the . . . what I've become. Your influence has been powerful, but it's a thin line I've been gnawing on. I've already broken through it more than once."

I briefly put my fingertips over his lips. "You know the maids? I'm the reason their tongues were cut out." That's not the worst of it, but I can't bring myself to recite my full list of crimes.

"Why don't you bite me and be done with it?" he snaps.

I keep my voice gentle. "Because that's not who we are."

Zachary wants to stop me, to keep me safe by his side. Obviously, he doesn't doubt that there's a heaven, so the problem must be . . . "I'm going to hell, aren't I?"

His answer won't change what has to be done. If not for me, then for every victim I'd take. For those I've already taken.

He clenches his fists. "I don't know. It's not up to me."

I shouldn't have asked. "Um." I glance at the empty reflecting pool. "I was planning this elegant moment with a *whoosh* and everything, but that's not happening."

Zachary doesn't reply.

"You said the way you tried to save me in the cemetery was a mistake. So long as it's my decision, will you make things right again? Will you set me free?"

It's too much to ask, but from the beginning, we've been in this together. Together, we have to see it through.

Somehow I know he can help, and that ultimately, he'll be glad he did.

"You're sure this is what you want?" he asks. "It's your own free will?"

What a strange question. "Yes."

Zachary's head drops for a moment, and when he raises it, his body begins to glow. He shows his wings, and I've never seen anyone more magnificent.

I take one step, then another, basking in his radiance. It's not always about reaching for heaven, I realize. Sometimes it's about heaven reaching for you.

The pain comes. It boils my cells and rips into my organs. Needles shoot through my body, into my skin, my throat, beneath my nails, into my eyes. My body shakes, and my teeth chatter. I hear a scream and recognize it as mine.

Zachary blurs into the golden glow, or perhaps it's me, blurring. With each step, my form grows lighter, and then the agony fades. It's too soon, though, too fast. He rushes closer — his lips on mine one last time. The light is everywhere. It fills me, fulfills me. I feel a last echo of pain, a last whisper of fear. "Zachary!"

I can't see him now. The shadows have come. I'm all alone in the dark.

Then suddenly, I'm rising, weightless, in a sea of black-and-blue butterflies.

The last earthly sound I hear is my angel's voice. He says, "Have faith."

Zachary

I DOUSE MY RADIANCE. I hide my wings. Miranda is gone. Her body disintegrated.

If an angel could die, what just happened would've killed me, too. I felt the pain pouring through her skin. I watched the spark fade from her blue eyes. I watched her burn to nothingness. I watched her vanish by my own light.

I could've said no. I could've insisted on fighting a losing battle alongside her. I could've held on to the last dwindling moments until the real her was gone. But that would've sacrificed us both and in a much more devastating way.

That night in the Dallas cemetery, I told myself I was doing the right thing for her when really it was about me. I wanted to hang on to her longer. I was selfish. Vampiric. I broke the rules and indulged myself at the possible expense of her soul.

No matter how hard it was, Miranda was right. Ending what Dracula did to her was the best way I could've shown my love.

I hear boots touch down. "Josh?"

It's the archangel. Michael. "Do you want to tell me what happened?" he asks, standing behind me.

"I don't want to talk about it. Besides, you already know." I shouldn't speak to him that way. Not Michael. Not that, at the moment, I care. I'm a failure. I failed Miranda. I failed the Big Boss. What more is there to say?

Then I turn, heartened, overjoyed to see the archangel cradling Miranda's sleeping soul. It's a transparent, sparkling blue echo of my girl.

"You did well," Michael announces. "You have fulfilled your mission."

Now I'm confused. "My mission?"

I think back to that conversation on the train. Josh said I was supposed to wipe out something of tremendous significance. Could he have meant Miranda? Was she the significant one?

Michael looks down at her spiritual form. "Yes, your mission. She has already given you your next one. Fulfill it, and you'll be welcomed back to heaven. Until then, earth is your home."

I struggle to unravel the grand scheme. My girl asked me to help save those vampires who could be redeemed. Michael just signed off on that. Since the beginning, such a thing would've been unthinkable. Angels had automatically written off the undead. But clearly, that's no longer the case. Miranda shifted the universe. She changed everything. And Michael's retrieving her soul means that she also saved herself.

Before I can thank him, they're gone.

My right hand falls to the hilt of a sword. My first thought is that I don't have a sword. Then I realize it's a gift from the archangel. I withdraw the weapon from its sheath and raise it, flaming, in the warm spring wind to the fading stars and rising sun.

I vow to honor my girl's wishes and take the challenge set before me. I vow to someday return upstairs to our community of heavenly beings and ascended souls.

I vow to be reunited with Miranda. No matter how long it takes, I can be patient.

After all, we have eternity.

AUTHOR'S NOTE

Dracula, the quintessential literary vampire, was created by an Irishman, Abraham "Bram" Stoker, in an 1897 novel by the same name. Three more of his characters, Jonathan Harker (along with his knife), Renfield, and Dr. Van Helsing, are also referenced herein.

This novel also was influenced by another classic, Charles Dickens's *A Tale of Two Cities* (1859), which members of my ninth-grade English class took turns reading aloud over the course of a semester.

Both books feature a character with variations of the same name, Stoker's Lucy Westenra and Dickens's Lucie Manette. This inspired my naming of Miranda's best friend. Two more of Dickens's characters are mentioned in passing: Madame Defarge and Sydney Carton, whose surname is attributed to a family plot at the fictional Dallas cemetery.

It also merits noting that Miranda's high-school play is *Romeo and Juliet*, by William Shakespeare. It's generally believed to have been written in the late 1500s. The story pays tribute to an even older tradition of tales of star-crossed and (usually) tragic lovers. Though Miranda and Zachary may be fairly placed in this category, their ending is more hopeful that that of Shakespeare's heroes.

Avid readers may also notice nods to the work of Howard Ashman, George Axelrod, "Blues Brother" Dan Aykroyd ("on a mission from God"), James Bridges, Frank Capra, Johnny Cash, Bob Clampett, Carlo Collodi, Walt Disney, John Fawcett, Neil Gaiman, William Goldman, Thomas Harris, Kimberly Willis Holt, James Howe, Bob Kane, John Landis, Aaron Latham, Arthur Laurents, Stan Lee, Alan Jay Lerner, C. S. Lewis, Frederick Loewe, George Lucas, Alan Menken, E. Nesbit, Sydney Newman, Pierre-Auguste Renoir, Anne Rice, Gene Roddenberry, J. K. Rowling, Jerry Siegel, George Bernard Shaw, Mary Shelley, Takashi Shimizu, Joe Shuster, Stephen Sommers, Stephen Susco, J. R. R. Tolkien, Leonardo da Vinci, Karen Walton, and Joss Whedon. However, *Wow the Crowd*, *Angels to Zombies: Apocalypse A to Z*, and the various vampire media outlets are entirely fictional.

Furthermore, the novel augments its settings with the occasional street, alley, building, business, or other fictional locale, most notably the vampire-controlled Whitby Estates on Chicago's North Shore. Likewise, it offers a fictional spin on a handful of historical figures who are mentioned in passing.

Finally, this story takes place earlier in the same universe as my novel *Tantalize*. Members of both casts will cross over in a forthcoming book, *Blessed*.

ACKNOWLEDGMENTS

Angels are everywhere!

I would like to thank: my agent, Ginger Knowlton; her assistant, Tracy Marchini; manuscript readers Greg Leitich Smith, Anne Bustard, Tim Crow, and Sean Petrie; and experts Brandee J. Hetle, Julie Lake, April Lurie, and Linda Mount.

I'd also like to thank the whole heavenly team at Candlewick Press for their faith, efforts, and professionalism, especially executive editor Deborah Wayshak, associate editor Jennifer Yoon, and intern Venus Musgrove.

Trouble brews when Quincie Morris and her uncle decide to remodel the family restaurant with a vampire theme. One month before the grand reopening the chef is mauled to death in the kitchen, and the murder suspect is … a werewolf!

Quincie has to transform Henry, the new chef, into Sanguini's vampire extraordinaire – and fast. But strange things are happening to her boyfriend, Kieren, and a deadly love triangle forms.

A dark, romantic fantasy – truly tantalizing.